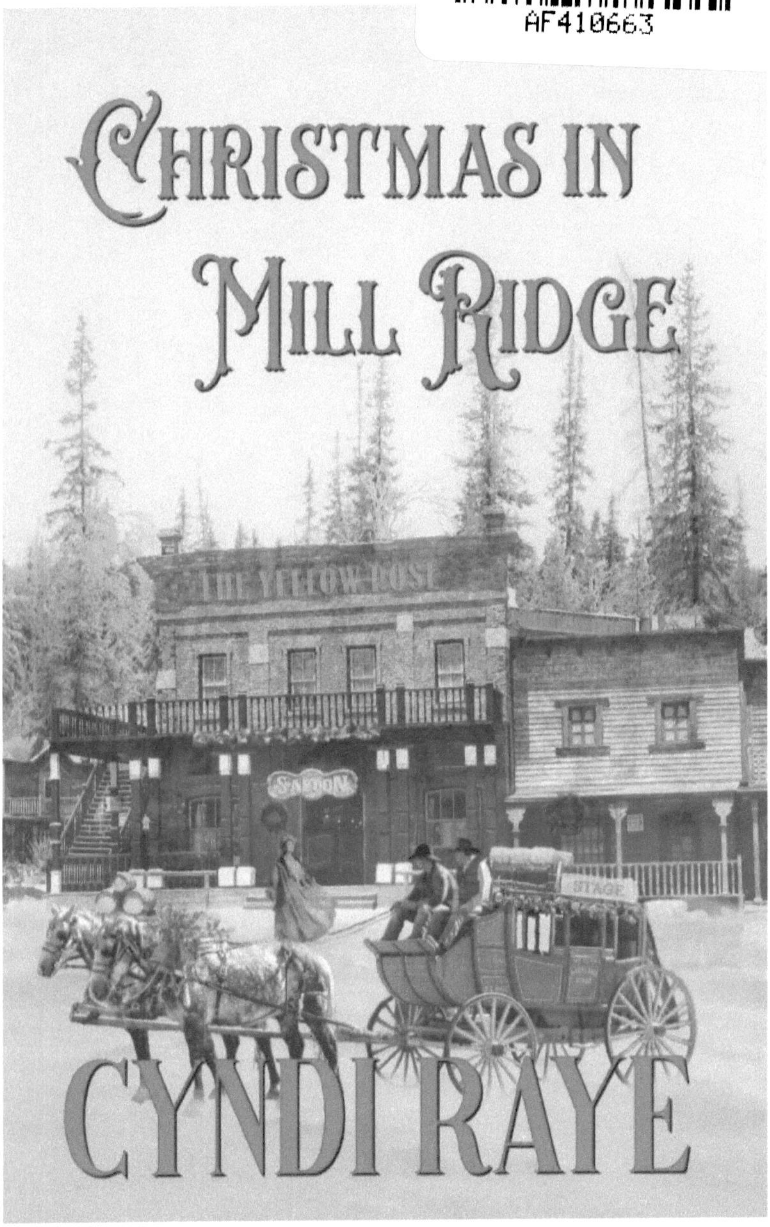
CHRISTMAS IN
MILL RIDGE
THE YELLOW ROSE
SALOON
STAGE
CYNDI RAYE

Brides of Mill Ridge Series Presents a Special Holiday Book:

Christmas in Mill Ridge
by
Cyndi Raye

---

1. http://www.CyndiRaye.com

Dedication

Thank you to my wonderful group of BETA readers for this book:
Sandy, Marcia, Tammy, Cindy E and Amanda! You girls rock and
I love the feedback in our little group!

Chapter 1

"Harridan!"

"I'm no such thing! How dare you?"

The man in the saddle leaned forward, one arm lying casually over the other. He held the reins loosely in his gloved hand. His wide-brimmed hat was cocked to one side shadowing the patch over his right eye. She immediately stared furiously at him.

"I dare say, Miss Steele. You walk around Mill Ridge so high-falutin' like you are above everyone else. Except we know you are just a parsimonious tempered woman with a sharp tongue and as mean as a rattlesnake!"

His words hit her full force. She pursed her lips like she was angry but he was right. She had studied her role well and her actions were always scrutinized. She knew exactly how people spoke of her behind her back. Most people whispered loud enough for her to hear and others tried to lower their voice in her presence. They turned away when she walked down the street. Which was precisely what she had wanted. It was easier to get by if people thought the worst and didn't try to get to know her. She had behaved the same way during her time with the National Teacher's Association.

Except he had the meaning of a harridan wrong. Which gave her a semblance of pleasure knowing she had it in her power to correct him. "I'll have you know, Captain Grayson Randall the third, that I am far from a harridan! If you would open the pages of a dictionary, you'd find out that a harridan is an old woman! Which I am not!" She raised her hands to her hips, tilted her head and gave him a condescending gaze that usually caused a man to shamefully accept defeat.

Not the captain!

He grinned.

Grinned like a little boy who got a train set for his birthday. Fury and hot steam boiled in her veins. He raised a brow above his one good eye. "That old plain brown dress you're floating in and large spectacles hanging from your nose make you look just like one. Your hair is plastered so tight against your head, it looks like your eyes are permanently squinted. I'm not wrong."

Erin deliberately pulled her hair back in a tight bun for her own personal reasons. He was a horrible man for bringing attention to her looks. The man had no soul! She would tell him so. "You, sir, have a black heart! Somewhere in time lies your black soul, being eaten alive by earthworms in the dirt. Captain Randall, you may go to that rotten place where the sun never shines!"

Erin's nostrils flared slightly as she turned her back and marched away. What else was she supposed to do? She had never walked away from a good debate, but his words caused her to feel ashamed of the way she looked even if she dressed this way on purpose.

Even though the noise from rickety wooden wagon wheels rolled past her, and several children ran by, their cries of joy reverberating through the air, the only sound Erin heard was the man's deep chuckle low in his throat. She turned back, her arms stiff and her hands fisted together but all she found was the backside of him and the tall horse he rode, moving down the street in the opposite direction.

Furious, she ran through their conversation several times before realizing she was at the general store. What was it about Captain Randall that had her blood boiling? Every single time they ran into each other since she moved to Mill Ridge two months ago, he'd been awful towards her. No gentleman should act that way!

Then again, the way she had scrutinized him the first time she met him probably started the whole thing. She tucked that memory away since she had a tinge of guilt over the fact she had not been kind to him at first either. Except, now he was taking it to a whole new level, calling her out in public when she wanted to just get by without anyone noticing.

Slipping through the front door of the mercantile was impossible, especially since Mr. Dunleavy's son attached an annoyingly loud bell to the entrance. The younger man was a nuisance. He followed her around the store, trying to be helpful, but she did not want someone breathing over her shoulder. How was she going to convince the people of Mill Ridge that all she wanted was to be left alone?

She had been sadly mistaken about this place. During her years working for the National Teachers Association, Erin had traveled near and far from her home in Tennessee. She had been sent to Mill Ridge and several surrounding towns to help promote education and make sure the teachers were acting accordingly as professionals.

Miss Jennie, Mill Ridge's beloved teacher, had troubled Erin from the start. She had been highly secretive and when Erin found her traipsing around with a Pinkerton agent, she had questioned the woman's association with him. Over time she had learned Miss Jennie was a valuable resource and Erin even came to enjoy her visits to Mill Ridge. No one would ever know that she had fallen in love with the place, since she deliberately kept everyone in town from getting to know her.

After the scandal, Erin knew this small town tucked away far from Tennessee was the perfect place to live without being noticed much. Her mother wouldn't be tempted to see the big city, like she had in Memphis. In a small town, Erin would be able to find her if she wandered away. But now, everyone wanted to mind her business and she just didn't have the gumption to focus on anything else but her mother.

That included Captain Randall.

"Miss Steele, hello. How are you this fine morning?" Ben Dunleavy's smile was so wide as he began to walk briskly towards her, waving his hand it startled her from her deep thoughts. She backed up a step without thinking and swung around to get away even though she knew he was just trying to be friendly.

Erin moved to the front of the store where the huge picture window showed the main street was bustling with activity. As she gazed through the window, a tall horse went by with a one-eyed man staring hard. He had a confused look on his face when he saw her at the window.

She took a deep breath, trying to compose herself. No one had ever looked right through her like the man outside just did. Even from a distance she felt his stare penetrate through her as if he knew all of her dark secrets from that one look. No one had or would ever see her vulnerability. That was not something she wanted to share with anyone, least of all Captain Randall.

Erin took her eyes off the captain and turned to Ben Dunleavy. Her chin went in the air and she cracked a tiny smile. Ben stopped in his tracks, surprise written all over his face. She thought maybe he felt his mission in life was to get the harridan to crack a smile. It almost made her giggle, but she held back.

"Is there anything I can help you find, Miss Steele?" he asked, his cheeks turning bright red.

"Not at the moment, thank you, sir."

"I can carry your basket for you, if you'd like," he offered.

Erin looked down. She had no basket. When she raised a brow at him, his face reddened even more and he stammered. "I, uh, am sorry. I was staring at you, Miss Steele and did not realize you had no basket. May I ask you if you would honor me with your presence this evening? A few of the merchants will be singing carols at the church tonight."

No one had ever asked her to do anything. In the two months she had lived here, everyone had either turned their heads or talked behind her back. Then, when they realized she wasn't going anywhere, and she was not going to have Miss Jennie fired, they were kinder to her, nodding and tipping hats to wish her a good morning or evening.

She rarely gave a smile to anyone, let alone a wave. Mostly, she nodded, and minded her own business. Erin didn't know how to answer Ben Dunleavy. "I can't," she sputtered before turning to the door and exiting in a very unladylike fashion. She turned towards home, almost running into a small child holding a basket.

Erin and her mother lived on Main Street, a few doors down from the teacher Miss Jennie and her husband Mack Everett. He was once a Pinkerton, now the town's deputy sheriff. At least her mother was safe being so close to men of authority. The sheriff's office was right up the street, they could see it from their own front porch. The first thing Erin noticed about the sheriff was how his beautiful wife came to visit faithfully every day. He'd wait on the front porch until he saw her and hold out his hand to help her inside. It was quite heart-warming, but Erin knew she'd never have a relationship like that. No one wanted a shrew! Or, a harridan, as the captain said.

It was probably soon time to have a serious discussion with him about her mother. Especially after the scare Erin had yesterday evening. She was about to push open the door when she heard the familiar clip-clop of a certain horses' hooves. Without turning, she felt the air begin to sizzle and knew it was the captain riding past. Did he know she lived here? Of course, he did. Everyone knew where the harridan lived!

She wasn't about to give him the satisfaction she noticed him and pushed open the door, stepping inside. Her mother usually sat in a wooden rocker at the window in the parlor, enjoying her view of the outside. Erin had made her promise not to step outside the house until she got back. They had a pact that when Erin returned, she'd take her for a nice, long walk.

Maybe her mother would enjoy going to church to sing tonight. She'd kept her away from most of the townsfolk, but perhaps she'd been doing her mother a disservice by keeping her holed up at home.

On the other hand, if the townsfolk knew how her mother behaved, they'd more than likely run Erin out of town without blinking an eye. It was a difficult decision to make, but perhaps she could give the town small doses of her mother. That might work. Besides, it was the holidays and her mother loved Christmastime.

"Mother, I'm home."

She didn't hear a sound. Usually, Erin would hear the wooden chair squeak as her mother groaned as she stood then rushed to give Erin a hug.

The room was empty.

Dread filled Erin from the top of her head to the tips of her kid boots. She rushed through the house, searching for her mother from room to room. Running up the stairs, she checked the two small rooms to find them empty. Erin quickly checked the back porch, hoping and praying her mother would be sitting on the stoop watching the birds.

She was not there.

Taking a deep breath, Erin marched across the room and pushed open the front door, leaving it hanging wide open as she hurried across the wooden porch onto the boarded walk. She turned towards the middle of town, not seeing anyone in a frilly blue dress. Erin always tried to dress her mother in bright colors since this had happened a lot back home and she was much easier to spot.

When she turned towards the sheriff's office, Erin noticed the captain's horse there. Dear Saints alive! Just what she didn't need right now! She swore if he called her one more name, she'd have him arrested for harassment. Erin turned towards the sheriff's office. She knew from experience that she needed help from the authorities.

A deep sense of failure eroded Erin's senses. She had been wrong to leave her mother alone. Even before they came here, her mother was showing signs of this demented stage of forgetfulness where she'd wander off aimlessly. Her father had begged Erin to come home and help him take care of her.

"Sheriff?" Erin pushed open the door of his office to find another bell jingling above her head. She frowned, knowing it would bring her undo attention when she walked through.

The two men were talking in low tones. The captain sat back in a chair that sat beside the sheriff's desk. His long legs were crossed casually in front of him while he lifted a small flask to his mouth, then handed it back to the sheriff, who promptly shoved the bottle in a drawer when he heard the bell go off.

He closed the drawer as if there was nothing out of order and nodded to Erin. "Miss Steele, is everything all right?" The sheriff had the decency to stand and take a few steps towards her, giving her his undivided attention.

She wrung her hands together. "I'm sorry to bother you, Sheriff, but my mother has escaped."

"Escaped?"

She nodded, totally aware she now had the captains attention too. Except he hadn't turned around to acknowledge her. She noticed the way his head moved slightly. He was listening, she knew. "Perhaps I should not say escaped, but is lost. My mother gets confused and wanders off. I don't know which way she went and thought it would be wise to have as much assistance as possible."

"Of course. I'd be happy to help."

Captain Randall stood. "I can help, too. I assume you don't want anyone in town to know of her state of mind."

Erin was surprised at his words. She was even more shocked that he offered to help after the way they had spoken to each other. It must have shown on her face. "Yes. I'd like to keep it as quiet as possible."

"I understand." He moved quickly, striding right past her as if she were no more than a post holding up the frame of the building and left. She watched out the window in awe as he lifted himself onto his horse. In a swift moment, the horse and rider moved quickly down the street.

She shook her head. "How does he even know what my mother looks like?"

The sheriff grunted. "Gray doesn't miss anything. I'm sure he saw her the day you both came to town and has her memorized in that craw of his. Let's go find your ma."

They hurried down the street, checking each alley in between houses. "She is wearing a bright blue dress with frilly lace and a bright yellow scarf around her neck."

"Like that one?" The sheriff pointed to her mother, who was standing on the porch of the boarding house, her leg over the railing and waving the bright yellow scarf in the air. Erin began to run towards her when she saw the captain slide from his saddle. He moved quietly towards her, speaking in a low tone. Her mother stared at the man, a look of fright at first.

Then she smiled at him. A wave of laughter bellowed from her mother's belly.

When Erin got closer she stood beside the captain and realized why he was laughing. "I will never let you forget this!"

He shook his head. "She's harmless and the pantaloons on her head have to be yours!" At that, his chest rumbled and white teeth she hadn't noticed before sparkled.

Erin was so embarrassed she could barely speak. "Mother, it's time to come home."

"No."

Erin was afraid of this. Mother was getting more difficult each time she ran off. "Please, Mother. It's time to make supper."

Her mother shook her head so hard it worried Erin. "No."

Erin noticed how her mother was smiling at the captain. She went to her side, trying to help her down from the railing. "Please, Mother. We need to go eat." Usually, food would convince her to follow Erin home.

"Not without this young, handsome man. You really need to be courted, Erin."

Erin felt the heat splattering across her cheeks. "Mother, please. It's -"

"I'd be obliged to accompany you and your lovely daughter to supper," Gray told her before they got into an argument. He held out his arm. Erin watched in amazement as her mother slid down from the rail and went to the captain. She put her arm through his and they began to walk towards home. The captain had her mother on one arm and the reins in his other, as the horse followed him down the street.

Erin stood frozen.

The sheriff's words startled her. "Looks like Gray has charmed your mother. It's probably best to be social until you can get your mother settled."

"How do you know I despise that man?"

"I've heard the conversations between the two of you. They are quite loud at times. I think everyone in town is betting on a Christmas wedding."

Erin's eyes bulged. "A what?"

The sheriff nodded. "Yes. With all that spark between the two of you, the whole town is betting on a marriage by Christmas."

"But didn't you hear what he said about me? He called me a harridan? Said I was a sharp-tongued something or other. He made me out to be the most horrible person in the world."

The sheriff laughed. "He sure doesn't know how to talk to a pretty lady."

Erin blushed. "Pretty? I'm far from that."

The sheriff shook his head. "Don't ever let my wife hear you say that. She likes to inspire women and she'd make it a point to help you discover yourself."

Erin thought about it and shook her head. "Thank you. Now, I better go. My mother can't be trusted."

The sheriff's hand shot out before she had a chance to take a step. He tipped his hat and looked right at her. "You don't have to worry about Gray. He's an honest man you can trust. He's also a man of honor."

"Thank you, Sheriff Nightengale. You don't have to worry, this is probably the first and last time he will ever be in my home."

She hurried home, making it a point to get the man out of her house before her mother invited him back. This was probably one of the worst things that had happened to them since they left home.

Every time her mother wandered off, the chance of the whole town knowing their business was more and more of a sure bet. She wanted to keep them unknown and to be left alone.

Erin knew it was almost impossible now. The eyes of the townsfolk were burning her back as she made her way to the house. Even though the sheriff would help, she knew sooner or later everyone would know and demand her mother be sent away.

She'd make a deal with the devil before she'd ever allow her mother to go to an asylum. This was her job. Her father had groomed her to be the one responsible to take over when he passed on. She was doing her duty as a daughter.

Erin wasn't going to allow anyone or anything to stand in her way.

Chapter 2

"Grayson Randall the third? What a distinguished name."

"You haven't told me yours?"

She smiled and accepted the chair he pulled out for her. Gray was hoping Miss Steele would be right behind him. He wasn't going to be able to stay much longer.

"How lovely. I am Mrs. Ruth Steele," the woman told him, a smile playing across her face.

"It's a pleasure to meet you, Mrs. Steele."

"Likewise. Please, have a seat. The servant will have our plates here shortly."

Servant? If Miss Steele heard what her mother said, she didn't mention it as she came through the door like a twister swirling across the prairie. She stopped dead in her tracks when noticing how the two of them sat casually at the table.

"Mr. Randall, thank you for escorting my mother home."

Gray chuckled. He noticed right away how out of breath she was with tendrils of hair falling lightly across her cheek. Wide, green eyes were assessing the situation. He noticed Miss Steele wasn't sure if her mother was going to be upset at the interruption or not. He knew exactly what she was going through. The turmoil inside of her had to be tremendous. Even though he understood, Gray thought she should learn a lesson about growling at a man the way she always did with him. "Would you serve our dinner, please?"

Gray watched as her cheeks reddened even more than they were and she opened her mouth, blinked, turned to her mother and looked back at him. In that instant, Gray knew she was aware of her mother's state of mind. Instead of giving him sass, Miss Steel tightened her mouth and gave a nod. "Certainly. Forgive me for getting home late."

A hiss came out of the elderly woman's mouth. "Don't let it happen again. Mr. Randall has been waiting patiently for his meal."

"I'm sorry, ma'am."

Gray watched as Miss Steele fled to the kitchen. He heard the rattling of dishes and something slam on the table. Then a loud groan came from around the corner and a crash so loud it made Ruth Steele jump. Her eyes were blank when he looked into them. She didn't have a clue her daughter was in the kitchen struggling to get supper for her.

Mrs. Steele leaned across the table. "I know she's incompetent, but don't worry. She can cook."

Another crash caused Gray to push his chair back. "If you'll wait here, I'll check on our meal. I'll be right back."

"That's a good boy," the older woman told him. She tore her eyes away from Gray and began to focus on the vase of fresh flowers on the table.

Gray reached the kitchen in time to keep Miss Steele from falling off a small stool she was balancing on. One foot was hanging over the side of the stool and the other was tottering on the edge. He caught her around the waist as the stool tipped over. "What are you doing?" he scolded.

The moment she fell into his arms, Gray forgot all about her mean temper. Or, the fact she had given him a what-for several times in the past month. Her mean-spirited talk had him thinking he was the last person in the world she wanted to talk to or get to know. Yet, there was excitement in the air whenever she was around. At least he had noticed it and enjoyed their bantering, even if she always walked away madder than a hornet ready to sting its prey.

He growled. It wasn't supposed to happen this way. Was this some kind of test? He liked her. But, she'd never want someone like him. He was told no one would ever care for a man with one eye. No woman in their right mind would want a man who was deformed and ugly.

Besides, she made it quite clear he was a nuisance and had a terrible attitude.

Then, why did he want to get to know her? She was warm and soft and felt just right in his arms.

Why did he yearn to kiss her?

He must be crazy!

Gray set her on her feet, backing away like someone was trying to place a spell on him. Why would he want to kiss this rude, fast-talking woman who gave him proper hang every time they met? She was not a nice person.

"Take your hands off me!" She sputtered like an old codger trying to eat an apple without its teeth.

"I'm not near you!"

"You were a moment ago." She ran a hand down her skirt, then pushed a few strands away from her face. The woman's red cheeks told him she wasn't as immune to his touch as he thought.

He was probably going to push the wrong buttons, but every time he was near this woman, something always happened. "A moment ago you looked like a woman who didn't mind being in my arms."

She turned, crossed her arms over her chest and puckered her mouth. Gray let out a deep growl. She needed to be kissed. He needed to be the man to do so. He took a step closer. Her eyes got huge.

"Wh-what are you doing?" She tried to back away but the cook-stove was in her way, which made him grin.

"I'm going to kiss you." There. He was going to kiss her come hell or high water.

"No. You are not." But, as strong as her words usually sounded, what came out of her mouth was a mere whisper.

He leaned in to take her mouth in his own, when someone tugged his sleeve. "Mister! You better have a good explanation for being in the kitchen with my daughter!" Mrs. Steele's voice sounded so formidable it caused Gray to turn away from the woman he was about to kiss.

The older woman was clearly deranged. "Yes, ma'am. I was making sure she was not hurt after we heard the crash from the dining room."

Mrs. Steele poked her head closer to his. Fire flashed in her eyes, reminding him of the way her daughter had done the same thing before. "You best be on your way, or I'll be sending for the preacher! No gentleman should be alone in the kitchen with my daughter. Do I need to go for my shotgun?"

Her words were concerning. He turned to Miss Steele. "Tell me you don't have a shotgun anywhere in this house?" he asked, his voice low.

She shook her head before taking her mother's arm. "Come on, Mother. Let's get you upstairs and ready for your supper. I'll help you."

"Thank you, dear."

The older woman looked over her shoulder with such a mean look, it had Gray heading for the door. He was getting out of this mad house! He let the door slam on his way out to make sure it latched and strode up the street, hoping to get home before his uncle wandered off.

"Where are you going in such a hurry?" Mack Everett, the newest deputy, asked. He was crossing the street towards Gray.

"To check on Uncle Frank."

"No need to hurry. I was just coming to get you when I saw you coming out of the Steele's home. Frank is at Mrs. Miller's place again."

Gray sighed. He used to be a proud man, married to his position as captain of his unit in the Texas Rangers. Now, he felt like he was losing his mind chasing after his demented uncle every day. "Thanks, Mack. I'll go after him."

The walk to the Miller's house at the edge of town didn't take long. Gray was weary and knew he needed some relief from taking care of his uncle, but times had been worse as a ranger. He'd go for weeks with hardly any sleep since the goal was to capture the criminal. This was a walk in the forest compared to his ranger days.

Except, he wasn't getting any younger and it was starting to wear on him. Not only physically, he could last all day chasing after the older man, but mentally it was causing him some foggy nights wondering what he had gotten into. Yet, there was no choice. He was the only relative left in the family. Gray was all his uncle had.

Uncle Frank had a knack for disappearing at the blink of an eye. When his aunt lay dying, she sent for Gray and made him promise not to let anything happen to Frank. Gray had made a bedside promise that day, knowing his days as a ranger were about to come to a halt.

His last jaunt as a ranger was helping his friend and comrade Grant Jennings a while back. Grant had sent for him to flush out a man who was after his wife, Mrs. Jennings. After that ordeal, his aunt had called him home and he knew what to do and where to take Frank to escape the eyes of townsfolk in their home-town when Frank would get angry and go after his neighbors for making fun of him.

They didn't understand that the man was not well. It was why he'd take items of clothing off his neighbor's wash line and sometimes wind up sleeping in their beds. Anger and resentment at his uncle was obvious and it was clear Gray had to get him away from those who did not understand the sickness. There had been talk of sending him to an asylum.

At the time, Gray wasn't sure what to do with his uncle until he remembered the small, restful town of Mill Ridge. It was perfect for Frank, so he sold the house and brought the man here. He rented a two-story house in town, but the more his uncle escaped, Gray was seriously thinking about moving him to a homestead outside of town where he wouldn't be able to bother people.

So far the people of Mill Ridge didn't seem to get angry when Frank wound up in their midst. Gray knew there would come a time when they did. He had seen it before. Yet, he worried that a homestead would be too lonely for Frank, who loved being in the limelight. It was a constant battle in Gray's mind. He had no clue what to do with the man.

Frank waved as Gray got closer to the Miller home. "Hi, son."

"Hi Uncle Frank. I thought we'd go to the café for supper. Are you ready?" He knew how much his uncle liked to socialize at the café. It was one of his favorite places to go.

Frank was sitting on the porch swing, reading a story to one of the Miller twins. He closed the book. "I'll be back again," he told the child, then followed Gray down the street.

Gray was a tall man, and he always had to look up to Frank. His uncle had once walked proudly, his shoulders back, an arrogant sway in his stride. Now, he shuffled more as the disease got worse. He still held himself proudly, but the doctor warned Gray that as time went on, he'd start to stoop and putting one foot in front of the other would get more difficult.

Gray sighed. He was deep in his thoughts when his uncle began to hurry down the street. Gray watched in surprise as the older man stopped in front of the café door and opened it for the two ladies about to enter. "I'd like to offer you both a place at my table," he told them, lifting a hand when the younger lady tried to argue. Frank shook his head. "You will be my guests."

From the corner of his good eye, he caught someone staring. When he focused more, he realized it was Miss Steele. He nodded, waiting for her to acknowledge him but she stared blankly ahead. Ok, now she was being too difficult. He walked closer. "Miss Steele, how interesting you decided to dine out this evening."

She turned her head away, walked through the door his uncle was holding open and promptly ignored his words. Gray grinned. What? No foul-mouthed remark came spewing from her? Where was that spit-fire he loved to exchange words with? He had to admit he liked her spunk.

Frank guided the two ladies to a large table and held the chair out for Mrs. Steele. Gray had no choice but to follow and do the same for the younger woman. She grunted instead of saying thank you. Yes, she grunted and he almost chuckled. She was not happy about the current situation at all.

He sat down beside her, placed the napkin on his lap and stared at his uncle who was speaking to Mrs. Steele. This was so odd dining with them without their permission, but his uncle must've already asked the older woman if they could. He hadn't heard the conversation since he was so busy staring at Miss Steele. When he looked at his uncle, the woman was laughing and encouraging him. The sparkle he noticed in his uncle's eyes was astounding. "I can't believe it," he murmured, not really speaking to anyone in particular.

"Neither can I. My mother is enthralled with Mr. Randall."

Gray realized Miss Steele was seeing her mother come alive for the first time, too. "I haven't seen him this calm and serene since his wife passed away. He's like another person right now."

"So is she." Miss Steele turned to him. "I don't like you. Not one bit. Even so, your uncle has a way of calming my mother."

Gray turned away from the old folks to stare back into those green eyes. They sparkled with a fury and confusion he understood too well. "I don't much care if you like me or not, but the two sitting across the table are getting on well, so don't spoil it by being a prude!"

Those green eyes flashed anger for a moment. She let out a deep sigh and agreed. "I'll do anything for my mother. She doesn't deserve this awful malady. The doctors call it morosis. All I know is her life is about to become more difficult."

Miss Steel was speaking in a low voice so her mother wouldn't be able to hear. She didn't realize her whole body was leaning closer to Gray. He saw the concern she had for her mother. "My uncle has the same issue. After I left your house, I found him sitting on someone's porch reading a children's story. I thought it would get better bringing him here, but now I'm second-guessing my decision."

Miss Steele tapped her fingernail against the tablecloth. "I would say it is good to know I'm not alone in this, but I don't wish this prognosis on anyone. I was hoping no one would notice when she tried to run off. I don't want to have to leave here because of her behavior."

"Mill Ridge is a decent place. Besides, it's almost Christmas and during the holidays it seems like everyone is of a kinder mindset."

Miss Steele nodded. "Everyone in town hates me. I don't want them to hate my mother."

Gray was surprised at her words. "I don't think people hate you, Miss Steele."

"You certainly haven't helped any." Her eyebrow rose in concern. "The way you scold me in front of everyone is preposterous. I've heard the talk behind my back."

"Talk behind your back? I've yet to hear any bad words about you." He grinned knowing it was a lie.

"Spinster! Harridan! Sharp-tongued! Your words did not help my reputation at all!"

Gray almost felt guilty. She had no qualms telling him how he misbehaved in her presence, so he was going to throw some back at her. "What about you? Accusing me of having a black heart and sending me to hell with the flash of your beautiful, round green eyes."

Those round green eyes flashed again, not in anger, but surprise. "Are you flirting with me?"

He gave her a long, drawn out look. "Maybe I am. So what?"

She harrumphed so loud it turned the heads of the older folks at their table. "Well, don't! I'm not interested in such things!"

Chapter 3

Erin wanted to get up from the wooden chair and run for her life. The man sitting at their table was rude, obnoxious and as handsome as the day was long. Plus, he was not here to make small talk or dine with her. He was sitting across from his uncle, making sure the older man didn't do anything out of line.

She was here because Erin didn't want her mother to become an embarrassment and cause them to leave town. Her mother wanted to go out to eat instead of cooking. Erin agreed only because she was tired. And she knew her mother needed to get out and about more often. It was bad enough having to move her away from everything the older woman knew, but then again, did her mother even remember anything about her old home-town or why they left?

Gray lifted a hand at her outburst and waved the people away who were sitting close by staring at their table. He leaned in closer. "You don't have to worry about your mother causing a scene. Look what your outburst did! Here comes the owner."

Erin spun around to see a plump, round woman no taller than a small child marching towards their table. "Howdy folks! I'm Evangeline Roberts, the owner of The Café. I bought this establishment from the previous owner who allowed ruckuses to go on. While I want you to visit my establishment, we don't allow outbursts of loud noises. Is everything all right?" Her round eyes stared right into Erin, knowing she was the one who had gotten loud.

"Oh, dear, Mrs. Roberts, I am so sorry. I thought there was a mouse at my foot and it startled me!"

Gray watched her closely, she felt him staring. The round woman's eyes widened so much Erin thought her forehead would disappear. "No, no, no, my goodness gracious! We don't have varmints in my café! Let me get you a meal on the house." She leaned in, smiling, but her eyes were worried. "Please do not call out again or I'll have everyone in town thinking there are mice all over the place."

Erin smiled. "Oh, no, ma'am, it was not a mouse. Mr. Randall accidentally kicked my foot with his big, clumsy boots!" She made sure to speak loudly so everyone heard. Erin did not want others to think the café had mice! She spoke out of turn, but hopefully her words would rectify her bad behavior.

A few gasps rent the air, then a chuckle or two followed. Gray shook his head and looked away.

"Was someone calling me?" the elder Randall asked, looking around completely unaware of his surroundings and the fact their table was the center of attention. He had a hand over her mother's and the two had missed the whole thing.

"Nothing to worry about, Mr. Randall. We were speaking to your nephew."

He nodded and went back to his conversation with Erin's mother. It was quite refreshing to watch her mother's eyes light up. She didn't want to disturb them again. "Please order the evening special for our parents," Erin told the owner. "We do not need a free meal. Mr. Randall will be happy to pay for it since he caused the disturbance."

The owner nodded graciously at him. "That's very kind of you, Mr. Randall." She left the table, hurrying back to the kitchen.

Mr. Randall grinned. "You think fast, I will admit. But now I think you owe me since you blamed this whole thing on me."

Erin smiled for the first time. "I don't owe you a thing, Mr. Randall. If anything, you owe me for not drawing attention to them." She gave the elders a stern look. "I haven't seen mother so happy in ages. They are good for each other."

"Too bad. That means I'll have to put up with you more often. Uncle Frank will want to see her every waking moment. At least I'll know where to find him. He'll be at your house with your mother."

Erin frowned. "I do not believe that would be appropriate unless they sit on the front porch."

"You tell them that. It's hard to convince my uncle of anything. When he is determined, nothing stands in his way."

"Hmm, like his nephew?" Erin smiled. From what she knew of Captain Randall the Third, and from the stories she heard around town, he had been a formidable enemy to those he hunted down while working as a Texas Ranger.

"Perhaps. Those days are long gone."

"Your legendary status lives on. I've heard so many stories about the great Captain Randall that when I did meet you a few months ago, those stories were hard to believe."

He lifted a brow. "Oh? How so? Why wouldn't you believe them?"

She tilted her head and watched him. He was leaning in, his elbow on the table. "Well, for one thing, you were not seven feet tall. You did not have a hook for an arm, either."

He laughed. "They thought I was Captain Hook?"

"I do believe so. But I knew you weren't a pirate at all. The sheriff told us how you helped Mr. Jennings, so now everyone thinks you are a hero. Some of the other stories are tall tales that circulate every time a new person comes to town. I've heard them all."

"I see. Well, many are probably not far from the truth." He seemed affronted that she accepted the fact most of the things people said about him were false.

She leaned back when one of the servers showed up with four heaping plates filled with steaming mashed potatoes, stewed chicken and biscuits. The younger woman set each plate down and moved away quickly.

Their meal was finished in silence. Erin looked at her mother to watch in astonishment as she ate her meal without prompting. She had been worried the plate would sit untouched. Mr. Randall had picked up her fork and filled it with food, then handed it to her. She took it, smiling and ate without being prompted. Erin did notice that the elder Mr. Randall hardly touched his own food.

"He doesn't eat much," Gray told her. "Mostly eggs in the morning is all I can get him to eat."

As he spoke the words, Erin's mother looked over and stared at the younger man. "We can't have that. I suggest a large slice of cake. Everyone eats cake!"

"That's sweet of you, dear. I'll have a slice, too."

Erin looked in surprise. "If he will eat cake, then let's get him some cake."

Four slices were served shortly after, along with a glass of milk for the elders. They ate with gusto and finished the glass of milk without a fuss.

Erin shook her head. "I have tried to get my mother to finish just one meal for months now. This is the best thing that has happened in ages."

"Same here," he told her. "Uncle Frank can go days without eating unless I prompt him to and then it's eggs, like I said."

She nodded. "I believe we have a common denominator; my mother and your uncle."

He grinned. "I guess so. We may as well push our differences aside and give them what they want. It will make both our lives easier."

Erin thought about what he said. She was exhausted taking care of her mother. Her days were filled with trying to keep the woman from running off, getting into something that would cause her harm. "I've been wanting to visit the school and see how Miss Jennie is faring. Perhaps I may bring my mother to visit with your uncle and vice versa. I'm certain you have things to do also. I'll be more than happy to give you a break."

At first Erin thought the man would refuse. There was something going on inside of him, as if he struggled with the thought of someone else caring for his uncle. Then, "Sure why not. I'd be delighted to have some time away when I don't have to worry. Every day when I leave him for a few minutes, he runs off. I know where to find him mostly, but it can get frustrating."

Erin nodded and leaned in. Without thinking she took the napkin in her lap and dabbed it along the side of his mouth where there was a small amount of icing.

Gray turned and stared at her with his good eye. It was brown in color with flecks of amber, and she noticed right away how sparkly it appeared. She almost grinned, knowing if she told him his eye had sparkles in it, he'd think she was crazy. He had been abrupt and rude with her before and she probably didn't help matters any, but now she was seeing a different side of him. Which made her feel slightly ashamed that she had also taunted him.

Why had she taken a napkin to the side of his mouth? It felt so natural to do so and yet she had no right. "I'm sorry, forgive me."

She quickly moved her hand back, but he reached out and caught her by the wrist.

"Don't be sorry. Not one bit."

Like a dark cloud covering the sky before the boom of thunder, Erin decided she had to get away from the wicked look in the man's eye. He was devastatingly handsome now that she had more time to take a better look at him. Which was not good. No, not at all. She moved her hand and pushed her chair back. "We had better be going."

Erin turned to her mother. "It's time to get home, Mother."

Frank stood and helped her mother out of the chair, holding his arm out for her. She smiled up at him, tucking her arm in his and the two strolled out of the café as if it were an everyday occurrence. Erin looked on in wonderment.

"It looks like we'll be spending a lot of time together, Miss Steele."

"I suppose so. They sure do look happy."

"I'd give anything to see that smile on his face every single day."

She turned back. "Anything? Even being civil to this harridan?"

He had the audacity to wink at her. "I'm pretty sure you aren't that miserable."

He began to walk towards the exit.

She followed alongside him.

He turned to her. She looked up and gave him a smile.

"Or, that old."

She smiled. He may not be so bad after all.

****

"Is my mother here with Frank by chance?"

He frowned. "Uncle Frank walked her home over an hour ago. He came back about twenty minutes ago and went straight to his room."

Erin began to get worried. She had been on the back porch shelling beans for tomorrow's supper when she heard the front door open and close. The hairs on her arms stood and she looked at Gray with huge eyes. "I believe he did walk her home. Mother told me she was going to sit on the porch until it was time for Frank to go home. I heard talking and took my time out back. When I came inside, it seemed eerily quiet so I peeked my head out the door to find the porch empty. I searched the whole house thinking Mother may have gone upstairs. She isn't in the house anywhere."

"I'm sorry, Miss Steele. Let me ask Uncle Frank."

Erin stood in the doorway, the front door hanging wide open. She was astute enough to know not to enter a man's home. She heard some noises behind her and turned around, hoping it was her mother.

Her face dropped when she realized it was Reverend Goodson and Nester Cravell from the Land and Title Agency. They had been talking quietly in front of the church when she crossed the street and asked them if they happened to see her mother.

"We came to see if we can be of help, Miss Steele. Have you found your mother?"

"I'm hoping she is here with Frank."

Reverend Goodson's eyes got so huge, the spectacles on his face looked small compared to the whites of his eyes. He pushed the wire frames back up his nose and sniffed. "That may be a problem if she is here with him without an escort."

Erin gave him a look of disgust. "There is nothing going on between Mr. Randall and my mother, I assure you, Reverend!" She knew it wasn't appropriate for her mother to be alone with Frank, but they were innocent. Weren't they?

Erin wasn't so sure as she watched Gray come down the stairs. Her mother was behind him and she twisted her neck to see her mother buttoning the top of her blouse. Oh, dear! This was not good. Maybe the reverend hadn't noticed. It was hard enough to see since Gray was so tall and had muscles rippling from everywhere. *Oh, stop, Erin! This is not proper behavior. Not at all!*

The frustration in the deep sigh Gray let out told Erin everything. When he saw Reverend Goodman standing at the bottom of the steps, he shook his head. "Can I help you, Reverend?"

The holy man pulled his shoulders back and shook his head. "We came here to help look for Miss Steele's mother, but it appears that there are some shenanigans going on here. Captain Randall, may I have a word with you in private?"

His uncle stood behind Erin's mother, a hand resting casually on her shoulder with a smile on his face. How could he possibly smile at a time like this?

Gray followed after the reverend. Erin stepped inside and stood alongside her mother, while Frank's hand stayed where he put it, not caring that Erin was staring at it hard. The door shut and they all waited silently while words were exchanged outside.

"I can't really hear what they are saying, dear."

"I can hear, my love. They believe you've been compromised and want me to make a decent woman out of you."

"I am a decent woman, what do they mean?"

Erin watched as Frank's hand left her mother's shoulder and he got down on one knee. "It means I wish to marry you, Ruth Steele, if you'll have me."

Erin's mother had tears in her eyes. "Of course I'll marry you. This is funny because I came over here thinking we were already married. But if you say we aren't and we have to get married, then yes. I will marry you again."

Erin wanted to close her eyes and pretend this was not happening. Her mother was so confused. The door swung open right as Frank stood and her mother wrapped her arms around his neck. Gray, the reverend and Nester Cravell stood watching.

Erin guided them out on the porch and closed the door behind her. "Now, listen here, Reverend Goodman! You caused a mess!"

"I caused a mess? It looks like both of your folks did, not me! You know we can't have your mother going into Captain Randall's house at will! My goodness, our town will get a terrible reputation again!"

"I understand that, but they are both innocent. He just asked my mother to marry him and she said yes! They can't take care of a household by themselves."

Gray shook his head. "There is no way those two can run a household and take care of each other. Why do you think I retired from the Rangers? My uncle was getting worse and he needed someone to stay with him. He can't be left on his own for long, something terrible will happen."

This was the first time Erin agreed with him. "The same with my mother. If we allow this to happen, they will probably harm each other one way or another. Someone needs to be with them to make sure they are safe."

The reverend stared first at Erin, then he turned his gaze to Gray. "Which one of you will take them both in?"

Erin stumbled a bit. "It's hard enough to take care of my mother. I can't imagine taking care of the two of them alone."

Gray nodded. "I'm afraid Miss Steele is right. Besides, I was considering buying a farm outside of town. That way if he wanders, it would be on my own land, not other people's homes."

Nester Cravell spoke up. "The Sterling farm is empty. Ten minutes ride from here. I can sell it to you right now and you can be in it by this evening."

Gray didn't hesitate. "If buying the land settles this, then consider it sold."

The reverend coughed. "I'm afraid that is not going to solve the issues at hand, sir. Miss Steele's mother was coming out of your uncle's room from upstairs. We can't have that nonsense in our town. They will have to be married in order for this to go away."

Erin spoke up. "He did offer to marry her. I watched him propose and my mother said yes." when Gray realized he would have to carry the burden of taking care of them both, he let out a long sigh.

"It is what it is, then. I'll deal with this. Nester, let me get my uncle and we'll stop by the Title Agency to buy the farm."

"I'll get the paperwork ready and meet you there," he told the captain, nodding to the others. At least he was happy, Erin thought to herself.

She turned to Gray. "Captain Randall, I won't let you do this by yourself. I'll come by every day and help take care of my mother. You don't have to worry."

Gray gave her a nod. "It's appreciated. I'm hoping on a farm, there will be plenty to do. I just have to fill it with chickens, and a few other farm animals."

The reverend shook his head. "Now, Miss Steele, you know you can't spend your days toiling at a farm that belongs to the Captain. What will people think? You'll be the talk of the town!"

Erin closed her eyes. This was not happening. "I never much cared what people think, Reverend Goodson. I know I'm not doing anything wrong. If others want to judge and behave badly, that goes with them, not me."

The reverend shook his finger. "It's not God's way! Besides, they'll write newspaper articles about your behavior and then other towns close by will pick up those articles and make the stories bigger than what they are. Soon, the good folks in Dallas will know about the lady in Mill Ridge who sneaks off to a farm owned by the famous Captain Randall. Do you realize the scandal this will cause?"

Erin hadn't thought about bringing attention to the town of Mill Ridge. She certainly didn't want attention for her mother. She paled. "I'm sorry, Reverend Goodson. I had no idea it would cause such a scandal." Now, she was worried. "What in the world will we do?"

Reverend Goodson reached inside his coat and pulled out his small bible. "There is only one possible way to fix this," he told her, staring hard. "You will also have to marry."

Erin frowned. "What?" Her voice was all but a whisper.

The reverend nodded. "I said you will have to marry Captain Randall and all these problems will be solved."

Chapter 4

Gray lugged the last of the items from the wagon onto the porch. He stood back, sighing deeply, staring at his new home, a white-washed, two-story farmhouse. A red barn sat a few feet away that housed two horses and a milk cow. A giant rooster, along with about a dozen chickens ran back and forth in the yard, pecking the ground where his uncle threw feed a short time ago.

Erin, his new wife, and her mother, were inside getting themselves settled. The last of their things had been brought here today. He was now a married man, thanks to Reverend Goodson forcing his hand.

Gray may be a son-of-a-gun to some, but he would not compromise a woman's virtue. It was why he agreed to this foolishness. The other reason was his uncle. There was no way he was able to take care of his uncle and Erin's mother both once the reverend caused the two elders to marry. His uncle alone was a huge handful.

Anger shot up and down his chest in waves. He didn't like to be forced to do anything let alone marry a woman he barely tolerated. If it wasn't for his uncle, he'd have left town and gone back to working as a ranger. Except, now that he was away from that life, it was nice not sleeping on the uncomfortably hard ground, or sneaking into a line shack on another man's ranch. He'd slip out before daylight, hoping a ranch hand with a shotgun wasn't close by.

There were times when he took those chances because he was sick of sleeping on the ground. Then again depending on the area, lying on the ground staring at a million stars was far better than a lonely, empty room. Where he wound up all depended on where he was and who he was trying to arrest.

Looking back, Gray realized he had been wanting to get away from that lifestyle for some time. He was good at what he did, enjoyed it for many years. Then, after Grant Jennings got hurt and settled in one spot, it made Gray want to find his own place to lay his head. He'd stare at the stars many nights wondering what it'd be like to have a family of his own.

Now, here he was, staring at that dream he wanted. Except, on the porch was a woman with her hair peeled back so tight and her hands on her hips in a fighting position staring him down like he was a little boy about to be reprimanded.

He walked towards her. "Mrs. Randall, what can I do for you?"

"Don't call me that!"

"It's your married name!"

Her green eyes squinted even more. "A name that was forced upon me. I swear you enjoyed it when I told the preacher where to go and he ordered me to hush my mouth and do what is right!"

Gray had to admit she was right. It had been quite amusing how angry she became when the reverend ordered her to do the right thing and marry him to keep everyone's reputation intact. She finally gave in but it wasn't before she threatened to let the whole town know that the reverend was sweet on old Mrs. Smith.

The reverend had paled at that and accused her of trying to blackmail him. She laughed in his face and told him that she had another plan up her sleeve and maybe he needed a taste of his own medicine. Gray had no doubt she was good on her word. She told the preacher he'd be as surprised as she had been when the time came.

Needless to say the quick ceremony Reverend Goodson held in the parlor of his house was short and quick. The reverend married his uncle and Mrs. Steele first and then the two of them. When he had taken Miss Steele's hand in his, it was shaking so much he had held it tighter. Her hand was enveloped in his and after a few moments he felt her calm down.

Even when she snapped out the words the reverend asked her to repeat, he knew she was not as upset as before. When it came time for a kiss to seal their marriage, she looked at the reverend and growled, then pushed her mouth against his cheek and left, taking her mother along.

That had been the longest night ever. Gray helped his uncle settle down after everyone left. Later, the two men walked to the Land and Title office to pay for the farm and get the new deed. His uncle was brooding. He did not understand why his new bride had to leave him. Gray had explained twice that they'd be together when they lived on the farm, but Frank just got angrier.

Gray knew there was not much more he could say. Frank would stew in anger until something else caught his attention and he'd forget temporarily what had happened. It was always like this. Tonight Gray didn't feel like dealing with Frank's frustrations but he knew there was no choice. He had promised to take care of his uncle no matter what. And, Gray never gave his word unless he meant it.

From the moment his bride and her mother showed up this morning, Gray's uncle had been the perfect gentleman. The transformation was incredible. The two were inseparable, now sitting on the rocker on the front porch holding hands.

But Gray's attention was on the snappy-mouthed woman staring him down like he was a prairie dog unable to find a hole to hide in. He looked up at her and grinned.

Her nostrils flared. She spun around and went inside, slamming the front door behind her.

"You got yourself a fierce-tempered woman there, son."

"Thanks, Uncle Frank. As if I didn't know."

"Now, now, you too. My daughter is a bit feisty but you don't have to call her names."

"I'm sorry, my love. Forgive me?"

The older woman batted her eyes, causing Gray to roll his own. He had a feeling her mother had been feisty in her own youth. He glanced at the two sitting in the rockers to find them enthralled once again at what the other was whispering. It was quite incredible the way the two had fallen instantly in love. He was happy for his uncle but having to marry Erin Steele in the long run was not to his liking.

Especially when she made it quite clear there would be no real marriage. He sighed and climbed the three steps to the wooden porch. The boards creaked under his boots. "I best get a hammer and nails and fix the steps."

"Young man? I'll have a list of other things for you to do as well. If you go inside and speak to my employee, she'll let you know what needs fixing."

Gray looked at his new aunt. A moment ago she was well aware Erin was her daughter. Now, her eyes were glazed over and he recognized the look. Frank was sitting beside her holding her hand, and nodding. He by-passed the two and pushed open the door. Clearly, this was going to be a long day.

When he got inside, Erin was putting dishes onto a shelf above the large sink. The kitchen was huge, with a big cooking stove, several tables and a huge wooden table pushed against the other side of the wall. There was a tall doorway to the parlor and the rest of the house and when Gray stepped through, he was impressed at the huge room in front of him.

He noticed the windows were quite tall and his first concern was replacing them if they got broken. Luckily, he noticed the shutters from the outside. If they had a bad storm, at least they would have the protection of the shutters.

Gray looked around the room. Wooden plank floors were nearly empty. A long settee sat between two windows and a rocker beside the couch. A huge fireplace was tucked against the outer wall where he was certain at one time was used for cooking. A rather large iron kettle still sat in the opening.

"I never saw such a huge fireplace before," his wife of one day retorted.

He nodded. "It looks like whoever owned this place after the original owners added the cook-stove in the kitchen. I believe this was the original kitchen."

She stood alongside him, staring at the fireplace. "I wouldn't have a clue how to cook with a kettle that size anyway."

"Lucky for you that you won't have to. Although it wouldn't hurt to learn."

She glared at him. He probably said the wrong thing. She had started the conversation pleasant enough but now she looked angry.

Gray turned to her. "I'm sorry, don't say anything. Let's let the older folks get adjusted before we start bickering back and forth.

I know you don't want this, everyone knows. After your words yesterday, we know how you feel about this whole situation."

She let her shoulders sag for a slight moment, then pulled them back and her chin came up. "I know this is best for the folks, but I do not like someone telling me what I have to do. When Reverend Goodson said it was for the good of mankind, I admit his words got under my craw."

"I agree,."

"You do?" She seemed surprised.

He nodded. "Yes. I made a promise to my aunt on her deathbed that I would take care of my uncle. That meant no matter what, I will make sure he is cared for and safe. It's why I left the Rangers."

"I see. That explains why you didn't holler back at me. You are braver than I am. It's still difficult for me at times, too. I guess it is for the best, Mr. Randall."

"My name is Grayson. You can call me Gray. After all, we are married now, if only in name."

She gave a nod. "Fair enough. You may call me Erin."

"Okay, thank you."

"To be honest. I don't want to argue and be miserly. But, sometimes, I think it is expected of me to behave that way."

Gray was confused. "Why would you behave that way deliberately?"

"I had a reputation to uphold. When I joined the Teacher's Association, every male at the Association laughed at me and said I was a dim-witted woman no one would pay any attention to. They told me that I was so pretty all anyone would notice was my beauty."

Gray stepped back in surprise. "Why would they say that? It's simply not true."

Erin's eyes popped open wide. "You need better manners, Gray. Of course you haven't seen my beauty. I do well to hide it from the world."

He came closer and stared into her eyes. "I see a spit-fire behind that façade, Erin. You are my wife now, so no one has to look upon your beauty except for me."

She stared at him a moment, a crease upon her brow. And then she gave him the biggest smile. "You are a genius and so right. You are my husband and now I don't have to hide from the world at all, do I? Maybe this arrangement has worked out for my benefit as well."

Gray was so confused at the conversation he shook his head. "I better go check on the folks." He left Erin in front of the fireplace and went back outside, his mind more perplexed than ever.

Chapter 5

Erin was satisfied at all the work she'd done in the last few hours. She had supper simmering on the cook-stove, the table was set and the freshly baked bread had been covered with a cloth. She found herself in the huge bedroom that she claimed earlier as her own. There were two bedrooms on the first floor and two upstairs. She wanted the one closest to the kitchen since she'd be doing most of the cooking.

Another reason she wanted the first floor bedroom closest to the kitchen was because of her mother. She had not been able to keep a steady hand for a long time now. Actually, the thought of her mother using a knife was terrifying. Many nights in their rental property, Erin found herself falling asleep in a chair close to the kitchen door in case her mother woke up and tried to make something for herself. It had happened quite often, mostly in spurts, but Erin was not taking any chances. There were more times than not that she had to sleep with one eye open.

Her mother and Gray's uncle had claimed the other bedroom, making it easy for the forgetful woman to wander to the kitchen at night. That left the two rooms upstairs for Gray to choose from. When he brought his carpet bag and set it on her bed, Erin shooed him out of the room and marched him upstairs. There was no way she was about to share a room with him with her mother next door, no matter that they were married.

He'd have to settle for the upstairs room. He reluctantly did so, giving her a hard look when she laughed at his surprise. It was more of a nervous laugh but she wasn't about to tell him so. The man did make her a bit nervous. Even if she had told him she wasn't going to consummate this marriage, a man like Gray was hard to say no to.

Yet, she'd have to. He was in this to help his uncle, not because he cared for Erin. She was aware of this when they exchanged vows. Well, as they were forced to exchange them. Just for spite, she should refuse to go to church on Sunday. That would show the reverend he can't run everyone's life.

Her petty thoughts had her smiling. There was no way she would defy the reverend. Everyone listened to him and most of the time he was right. Except for this time. No one had done anything wrong. But, she was glad her mother was settling down now that she was married to Frank. How long it would last, no one really knew. At least everyone was all together on this farm and they wouldn't be able to wander into other people's homes.

There were many times when her mother looked at Erin with a distant stare. It had been awful at first, knowing the woman's mind was going. She knew someday her mother would not recognize her at all and then she'd never have her back again. The doctor told her to expect it to happen. The sadness she felt knowing her mother would never be the same again brought a tear to her eyes. Why did such a terrible thing have to happen like this?

As far as the doctor said, there was no known cure. It happened to some people and others were fine. He also told her that it would get a lot worse, so try to enjoy the time they had left. Erin closed her eyes. She didn't want to think that far ahead.

She gazed into the mirror above the dresser, a small oval glass encased in a wooden frame. The owner of the farm had left everything behind. Erin wondered why. She'd have to ask Gray if he knew the reason or what happened to abandon such a beautiful piece of property. It was awkward using someone else's belongings and yet they had needed the items. Erin had a feeling Gray used most of his savings to buy this farm.

He didn't know she had money tucked away in savings. No one did. Well, the banker knew but that was no one's business. When the scandal occurred a few years back, before she became involved with the Teacher's Association, Erin had made up her mind she'd never depend on anyone but herself. So far she had been lucky enough to save her money since the Teacher's Association paid for her travel expenses for years, leaving her to stash away every penny she earned.

When she had to leave the association to take care of her mother, she had used her parents money first. There was still some left but it began to dwindle fast when she got to Mill Ridge and had to start paying rent. Now, living here on the farm, she'd hopefully be able to keep both savings intact in case she ever had to make a quick getaway.

Someday she knew she'd have to leave. After this horrible disease takes her mother, there would be no use for someone like her. Erin knew it and would be prepared. Her hand slid to the knot on her hair. She loosened it, a bit nervously, allowing the soft tendrils of hair to fall across her shoulders. For the past few years, she had worn her hair so tight it sometimes gave her a headache. Perhaps, it was time to free it for a bit. After all, there was no one here on the farm to see her. There was no one to make fun of her or accuse her of anything here. Gray certainly would never notice how she looked.

There would be no one to notice her blind beauty, as that man had called it. She stared long and hard at herself in the mirror and smiled. The smile softened her face, causing her eyes to sparkle. She knew she had the most beautiful eyes, but her thick spectacles hid them quite well. She slid them off her nose and laid the dark rimmed glasses on her dresser. The truth was, she didn't need them at all.

This was her first supper as a married woman. She truly wanted to free herself from the suppression she had felt for the last few years. Erin had known no one would look at her twice the way she had presented herself and she had been right. People left her alone, thinking she was a spinster or worse, a harridan.

After what that man had done and said to her, she was afraid to ever try to feel pretty again. Yet, she stood in front of the mirror, wanting the one thing she had tried to hide from; her beauty. The ache in her soul was too great. Maybe it was because of Gray, she wasn't sure. Erin slowly pulled the rest of the pins from her hair, letting them drop onto the hard wood.

A pounding began on her door. "Erin, are you in there?"

Gray! His deep voice caused her to jump in the air. The hair brush she just picked up, fell to the floor, making a clattering sound at her feet. She grabbed her glasses, shoving them onto her face. Pushing her hair back, she hurried to the door. "I'll be right out."

She heard his boots hitting the hard floor as he turned around and left. Erin let out a deep sigh. Why was she so nervous? It was silly and yet she felt all shy when he was near. Which was ridiculous because they could not stand each other most of the time!

With those thoughts, she turned the knob and pulled open the door, determined to make this work. She pressed her hands over her plain brown dress and straightened the apron, ignoring the stares from her mother and Frank as she entered the kitchen.

The two were sitting at the table as if they were in a restaurant waiting to be served. It almost made Erin smile. "I'll have supper ready in one minute," she told them.

Gray came around the corner and stopped in his tracks. She felt his eyes on her as she picked up the pot of stewed beef and dumplings. He watched as she set the pot on the table, then went back for the fresh bread. "Are you going to sit down and eat?" she asked him.

"I'll wait for you," he told her.

"How kind of you," she said, unable to look him in the eye. Leaving her hair loose was a huge undertaking for Erin, even though no one had said anything about it yet.

When she took off her apron and hung it on the hook by the cookstove, Gray moved to her chair, pulled it out and waited for her to be seated. She gave him a small thank you while he sat at the head of the table. They bowed their heads for a prayer, which he led. The moment he said amen, Frank's hand reached for the pot. He ladled a spoon for his wife then commenced to fill the other bowls as well.

"Thank you, Frank. That is kind of you to serve," Erin told him.

"It is my duty as the elder of this family." He stared at Erin for a moment, his brow creased. "Why, you look different tonight, young lady. I can't put my finger on what it is, but you look soft."

Erin lowered her lashes. *Soft!* She had never been called that before. Hoping Gray was too busy eating, she peeked at him and was glad he was staring at his bowl of food.

It was almost forgotten until her mother chimed in. "Frank, don't you remember how lovely Erin looked before that scandal? Why, if it hadn't been for that awful man, she'd have never covered up her eyes or pulled her hair back the way she does. Don't you remember?"

Erin stilled. The scandal was not something she wanted to explain to anyone else.

"No, I don't believe we knew each other then, my love."

"Oh, dear! You just don't remember! It was during the holidays. The Langley Christmas Ball. Erin was dressed up in that gown and looked so beautiful until that man attacked her on the veranda! Luckily, you stopped him before anything bad happened. But, it was too late. Erin-"

"Mother, please!" Erin shot out of her chair. "I need some air," she cried out, then made her way to the front door, across the wooden porch and down the steps. The moment her feet hit the ground, she began to run. That's when deep sobs burst in the air. Erin didn't realize she was the one crying out. The memory of that night was so raw and real that it had propelled her to run across the yard so fast that when she did stop and notice her surroundings, she stood at the end of their property.

A large limb was lying on the ground, smashed against another fallen one. Erin sat on the thick tree limb, her face in her hands, her shoulders shaking as she tried to get herself calmed down. She took in short, deep breaths and let them out slowly.

A shadow fell over her and she knew it was Gray. "You have no business following me," she told him, her voice shaking, gasping for more air.

"You are my wife, whether you like it or not. I'm responsible for you."

She kept her eyes closed for a moment. Of course she would be his responsibility. "I'm sorry for behaving badly."

Gray stood his ground, towering over her. "From the way it sounded, you had a good reason to be upset."

She looked up at him then, realizing he wasn't trying to boss her around or tell her that she didn't have the right to disclose her feelings. This was quite different than what she expected from a husband. "You are causing my neck to strain standing over me like that. Here, sit." She scooted over to give him room.

Gray sat, his long legs stretched out before him, elbows resting on his thighs. He leaned over and gave her a sincere smile. Again, she was quite surprised. After all, she wasn't really a true wife in the sense he had to act as if he cared about her. Yet, he was showing her undivided attention. She was not used to that.

"If you don't want to talk about it, you don't have to. As your husband, I'll go find the son-of-a-gun that hurt you and give him a talking to. Will that make you feel better?"

Erin was amazed and shocked. He didn't ask what happened or want to know details. He didn't accuse her of causing the scandal like so many of the others did at the Langley Ball, including the Langleys themselves.

Instead, he accepted her word that she had been upset by the whole thing and thought the right thing to do was to go after the man who caused her grief. "I don't know how to answer that, Gray." Her voice was soft, barely a whisper as she looked up at him.

"I don't know what happened, nor do I care to know. It's your private business that happened before we were wed. But, if the past causes you this much pain, then I want to help you make it better. If you can hold down the farm, I'll be on my way in the morning to confront this fellow that harmed you."

She was confused. "You'd do that for me? What if I were the one that caused this all? I may be the one to blame."

He shook his head. "That's not the issue. He compromised you. Has he ever been punished for the harm he has done?"

She looked away. Too quickly, perhaps.

"Erin, tell me. Was the man punished?"

Her heart rate went up. She felt the erratic beating in her chest. Her throat became dry. It was all coming back to her. Erin had tucked all the emotions from that day deep in her soul and now it was rising to the top.

"Erin, please. Don't cry."

She felt his arm around her shoulder and she didn't pull away when he brought her to his chest. It was a good feeling, a safe haven for her dreadful demons. The warmth from his body enveloped her like a cloud covering the sun on a day that was too humid. He began to rock her gently, as if she needed the motion.

He was right.

She did.

The rocking stopped when she spoke again. "I won't cry, Gray. You don't have to go after anyone. The man is dead."

Chapter 6

Dead? The conviction in her voice made him pause. Had she been responsible for the man's demise? If the truth be told, the man was lucky it was her and not him that killed him. He began to rock her again, enjoying the quiet of the evening. It had been hectic the last few days after the so-called marriages.

Now, with the old folks settled in the house, he was able to breath some fresh air and talk to his wife. He wanted to know what had happened to her, but her soft, wavy hair lay against his arm and it felt so nice. Like the goose-down pillows he'd experienced in a Kansas hotel room after a month-long journey of sleeping on the ground. Gray leaned back against the tree, taking her with him and looked up at the sky with his one good eye.

"We're all flawed, Erin. No one is perfect. Look at me. I have one good eye and yet I never thought I'd be where I am today."

She stirred in his arms, and looked up at the same sky. The sun had gone behind the clouds a while ago, causing the air to become a degree cooler. Dusk was close at hand. She spoke softly. "I know how people talk about me. Wherever I go, even if people don't know about the scandal, they still talk. I do it on purpose, you know."

He chuckled. "I do know that underneath that hard demeanor you are a soft woman that longs for love, just like the rest of us."

She turned in his arms, her eyes flashing. "What do you know of that? I've never once shown anyone that I can be a nice person! The whole town of Mill Ridge thinks of me as a shrew. The truth is, I want them to believe it. People need to stay away from me. I caused my father to kill a man!"

Her eyes filled with unshed tears as she stared at him in horror.

"Is that what you believe?" he asked.

"Yes. It's true. Mother told me after it happened that if I wasn't so beautiful the man would've never laid a hand on me. She said it was my fault father went to jail."

Gray wanted to be angry at her mother, but sadly, the woman probably didn't remember anyway. "That's simply not true, Erin. A man is responsible for his own actions."

"Not according to my mother or the town of Memphis. I was told over and over again that I was the one at fault. At least up until the trial. He sat in jail for a month before they let him go on the grounds of self-defense. There was no self-defense, Gray. My father was so angry, he marched up to the man and shot him in the chest."

The tears that had pooled in her eyes released. He took his fingers and gingerly wiped them away. Cupping her cheek in his palm, he forced her to look at him. "Erin, it's time you stop blaming yourself. Your father did what any decent man would do. He was protecting his own."

"Mother doesn't remember taunting me about it. After he was out of jail, I took a job with the Teacher's Association, changed the way I looked and never looked back. My father wrote me a letter once, asking me to promise to take care of mother because he was ill and didn't think he'd be around too much longer. That's when I went home to find him dying."

"I'm sure most people had forgotten by then what happened."

Erin shook her head. "No, it started again at my father's funeral. Several of the Langley family were there, and blamed my father's early demise on me, too. This time I was strong-willed enough to have them escorted out of the graveside service. Soon after, mother and I came here, to Mill Ridge. I wanted a fresh start after talking with her doctor."

"I'll admit you leave quite an impression behind. Let's start over, Erin. We both know this marriage was something that neither one of us wanted. Yet, here we are, knowing it's for the best for your mother and my uncle. I don't take promises to others or myself lightly. I am a man of honor, Erin. Maybe we had to marry under the circumstances that befell us, but I'll stand behind this marriage, if you will."

She closed her eyes. He stared down at her, wondering if she'd get up and walk away. "I'll try," she told him, then sat up, removing his arm from around her shoulders. Erin sighed. "I don't know how to be a wife, or be pretty, or make someone happy. I've worked so hard at being so miserable that I don't honestly see how anyone would want to be around me, let alone be married to me."

He grinned. "Ah, Erin. You have no idea how beautiful you truly are."

She grimaced. "I don't want to be beautiful, Gray. Not anymore."

"You can't change how you look."

She shook her head. "Yes, I can. I did."

Gray helped her up when he saw her struggling. He stood and held out his hand. "I only saw a sharp-toothed woman with the most lovely green eyes snapping at me like she was going to tear me into a thousand pieces. Your spunk made me want to pull you into my arms and kiss that mouth of yours until it was red and puffy from my kisses."

"Gray? How can you say that? My hair was plastered back and I knew I was not attractive at all. I did it on purpose so no man would ever want to kiss me again."

"Sometimes a man with one eye can see better than one with two good eyes."

She gave him a smile that lit up her face. 'Thank you."

"You really are pretty, Erin. I knew that if you took down that hideous bun, those soft-spun curls would be soft." He gathered some of her hair in his fist and ran it through his fingers.

She froze. "I'm not used to so much attention."

"Get used to it, Erin. I want to show you that not every man is like the one who -"

She shook her head. "Please, Gray. I can't talk about him."

Gray grew frustrated. It was time to be straight forward and force her to face the truth. "Erin, you will never get over the scandal if you don't face your demons. This man, he tried to force his way with you. Tell me what he did. Talk to me, Erin."

She stayed silent at first. "No one ever asked me how I felt, or what happened. They all assumed it was my fault. It wasn't, Gray. He asked me to dance at the ball. I was having fun dancing and enjoying myself. It was Christmas eve."

"As you should. I imagine it was quite exciting for you."

She nodded. "It was at first. I felt like the most beautiful woman there."

He leaned in and whispered in her ear. "I'm betting you were the most beautiful woman there."

She blushed. He felt her relax some. "Tell me what happened, Erin." At first, he didn't think she was going to until she let out a small sigh.

"I was dancing with a cousin of the Langleys when he started dancing and guiding me towards the gardens. I didn't think it would hurt to go to the gardens with him as he was a gentleman. Once there, Thomas began to kiss me so hard on the mouth, I tried to push him away."

She began to shiver. Gray took her hand. "Tell me, Erin. You will feel better once it's out in the open. I won't judge you."

She shook her head slightly as if she wanted to forget. Then, it all came out in one huge flood. "Once I pushed him back, I saw the flash of anger in his eyes. He growled at me and told me that it wasn't nice to refuse someone like him. He said if I didn't do what he wanted, he would accuse me of trying to steal the ring he had on his finger, and have my whole family thrown out of town."

Gray felt the anger burning inside of him at the man's sinister tactic to try to blackmail someone.

"At first, I was scared. I let him kiss me again because I didn't want to get into trouble and I didn't want my family to think I stole something. But when he pushed his tongue in my mouth and grabbed my chest and tried to pull my gown away, I slapped him so hard he fell into one of the plants close by. I tried to pull away when my gown tore. He held a chunk of fabric in his hand. It was horrible. The noise he made as he began to scream at me was agonizing and terrible."

"I'm sorry." Gray wanted to pull her close but he knew she had to get it out without interruption. No gentleman behaved like that, only heathens. Sometimes those ballrooms were wilder than the wildest west.

"I ran and found my parents, who were on the other side of the ballroom. When they saw what happened, my father was livid. He went outside to the gardens and we heard a shot. That's all I remember. I knew my father killed him without blinking an eye. Everyone there said when my father confronted him, he lunged himself at my father. But, I knew the pistol was already in my father's hand when he walked away from me. He had every intention of putting a bullet through that man."

Gray didn't blame her father one bit. If he had a child and she was compromised, he'd have done the same. Shame on her mother for blaming Erin. Gray finally spoke up. "It doesn't matter if he had his pistol at the ready when he walked away from you, Erin. That does not mean he would've shot him. You can't blame yourself. The situation got out of control and what happened was fate. No one can be blamed for that."

"I carried this blame for so long, I honestly do not know how to get rid of it. I want to, I truly do. I just don't know how."

He felt her arms go around his waist. It felt nice. "I'll help you, Erin. I promise."

"Right now, I feel like you will. Thank you for not judging me or blaming me, Gray. You are right, it feels a little better now that I don't have this burden to carry in silence."

He wrapped his arms around her, careful not to hold her too tight and scare her off. "If I have to spend the rest of our lives convincing you that you are worthy, beautiful and innocent, I will do my best to make you believe it."

She tried to step back. "I'm not sure I believe you. I know we got married for the elder's sake. When that responsibility ends, I'm afraid you may not want to be attached to someone like me."

Gray knew it wasn't going to be easy convincing her she was worthy of happiness. He'd have to show her instead. "Let's worry about - what the hell is going on?"

They both turned to the porch, where the screen door was flung open and smoke billowed out. Two bodies stumbled onto the porch until Frank took a hold of Ruth and pulled her down the steps. They both tumbled to the ground, coughing and hacking at the top of their lungs.

Gray ran towards the house, overstepping chickens that squawked as he stepped over them. He heard the sway of skirts and knew Erin wasn't far behind. "Take care of the folks!" he ordered, before taking the steps two at a time and ran into the house head on. The smoke was intense. He pulled at his shirt, tearing the buttons off haphazardly, then flinging his arms out of the sleeves and shoving the cloth around his mouth and nose.

The smoke was thick causing his one good eye to water. It was hard to find the source of the smoke until he saw where it was coming from. The oven door to the cook stove was partially opened, with smoke billowing from there, causing the kitchen to smoke up. A partial piece of cloth was sticking out. Gray took the broom from the corner of the room and pushed open the oven door.

A burst of smoke followed as the air hit the inside of the oven, but he was prepared. Gray's shirt was secured tightly around his face, while he pushed the handle of the broom into the stove to drag out the cause of the fire.

It plopped to the ground, all that was left was a sleeve. Someone put a coat in the cook stove. Gray wasn't sure whose coat it was, but at that point he needed to get it to the water trough outside. He pushed the cook stove closed and tightened the handle with his shirt, immediately causing the smoke left to go up the chimney.

Gray picked up the sleeve with the handle of the broom and carried it outside, dropping it at the water pump. He used the handle to pump water onto it. It sizzled as the cold spring water made contact.

He looked up to find Erin watching him closely. The two elders were still sitting in the yard, coughing quietly. His uncle was rubbing Ruth's back, leaning closer and talking softly asking if she was okay.

Erin watched Gray as he picked up the sleeve from the water trough. "Who put this in the oven?"

Ruth looked guilty but she denied doing anything.

Erin had a grave look on her face. "Mother, did you put my coat in the cook stove?"

"I, oh, I don't recall!"

Erin stared at her mother. At first Gray thought she was going to reprimand the older woman. Then, Erin sat down in the grass beside her and spoke softly. "Were you trying to clean my coat, Mother?"

Ruth nodded. "It was hanging on the hook and when I went to leave the kitchen I thought maybe it would need to be put in the wardrobe. I didn't know the wardrobe would catch on fire!"

Erin nodded. "Don't worry. We'll sit on the porch and have some lemonade. I know you like lemonade, Mother. What about you, Frank. Would you like a glass?"

"I'd love a glass. It's my favorite!"

Gray wasn't one bit happy. Every time he got short-tempered with his uncle, he tried to remember his promise to take care of Frank. It usually worked, but this time the danger was obvious. Nothing like this ever happened before. What if they had been farther away? The house may have burned down. How did Erin stay so calm and offer lemonade when all he wanted to do was shake them both for their foolishness.

He gritted his teeth together as Erin helped the two from the ground. "Let's go to the porch, where there's a nice breeze and the fresh air will cleanse the lungs," she told them, smiling like they were going on a picnic.

She walked by him, and smiled. Smiled! Gray's nostrils flared and he was about to say something, when she raised a finger and placed it against his mouth, causing a sensation to stir from deep within his soul. "We're having lemonade. Would you like to sit with us and have a glass, Gray?"

She didn't wait for an answer, but moved the older folks to the porch, where she settled them in and then casually went into the house. Gray didn't know if he should follow her or go sit on the porch. So, he stayed right where he was, making sure the two on the porch behaved.

He just watched an angel change his whole world as he knew it. She was amazing, smart and practical. Her beauty was not only from the outside, but there was an inner beauty that was slowly working its way out.

Gray wanted to be the one to see her spread her wings like a butterfly.

Chapter 7

It was clear to Erin that Gray wanted to reprimand his uncle for almost starting the house on fire. Luckily, the stove was the only thing affected. The air in the kitchen was pretty well cleared out, but the after effects of a smoke-filled room caused Erin to cough. Her throat became dry and she quickly made a fresh batch of lemonade.

It was one of her favorite drinks and her mother never refused a glass. Erin made sure to keep fresh lemons in stock at all times. The first time she went to the mercantile and asked for fresh lemons, the look on Mr. Dunleavy's face was disturbing. When she had collected her items and went out the door, she heard him tell one of his customers she was as sour as the lemons she just bought.

Back then, it pleased her because she knew she had done her job of becoming a miserable harpy. The unkind words had always bounced off of her shoulders. She had wanted that reputation to stick.

Until now.

Perhaps she had been too hard on herself all along.

Taking the tray of drinks outside, Erin passed the tray around, watching the delight on her mother and Frank's faces as they enjoyed a glass of refreshing lemonade. Even though it was mid-December, it didn't stop her from making the summer drink this time of year. She walked to the edge of the porch where Gray stood, leaning against the railing. "Would you care for a glass, Gray?"

He picked one from the tray, taking a long slug and wiped his mouth with the back of his hand. Then he finished and set the empty glass on the tray. "Thank you, Erin. I have some work to do in the barn." He promptly turned and began to walk towards the huge building, to which he turned to her and grinned. "You need a new dress."

"I need a new dress? What? Where did that come from?"

He shrugged. He faded into the darkness as the sun went down. "You can't go to church in that!"

She looked down at her dress, then up at his amused face. "I have been attending church in this dress for months now!" Erin still stood there, her hands holding the tray.

"You are married to me now!"

She frowned. "What does that have to do with wearing this dress on Sunday?"

He walked backwards, still grinning. "No wife of mine will be seen in rags. It's time to show off my angel in a dress to match her beauty."

The compliment made her blush. Was he talking like that to make her feel better, knowing what had happened before? He was being thoughtful but she didn't want to please the townsfolk. Not any more. She'd rather live out here on the farm and never go to town. "I'm happy not to go at all!"

"Nope. That won't happen either. Now that I know how beautiful you are, I want the whole world to see you with your hair down. Either you go get some material for a new dress, or I will!"

Erin was quite shocked and even more pleased at his words. "If you insist, I'll go and take mother with me in the morning. Can you keep Frank occupied while we are gone?"

"Nope. I'll take you both. I'm sure Uncle Frank wants to pick up some things in town."

"Thank you," she muttered, not realizing he heard.

"Your welcome, Erin." His voice was low and he stared at her with his one good eye. She stared back, wondering what he looked like without that patch over his face. It didn't matter to her. She knew flawed well, and she'd seen the man behind that patch these last few days. No wonder he was a great ranger.

"Are we going to make you a new dress, dear?"

"Yes, mother. We have to go buy material tomorrow. Will you help me sew it?"

"Of course. Did you see the mechanical sewing machine inside, dear?"

"Is that what is sitting in the corner of the parlor, Mother?" She had recognized the large wooden contraption as such, but never thought about using it. The prior owners had left it behind, along with everything else.

"Yes, dear. I saw a demonstration once in Memphis. You use your feet to work the machine and to help turn the wheel. I'll show you."

After everyone was tucked in bed, Erin sat staring out the window of her room. The moon was bright enough that it lit up the night, along with a thousand tiny stars. A light tap on her open door had her turning her head. She didn't dare close her door in case her mother wandered during the night.

"I locked all the doors. Put the key on the ledge above the door frame in case you need it," Gray told her. He peeked his head around the corner, but was polite not to look at her in her dressing gown. "I doubt the elders can reach that high. If they try to drag a chair to the door, I'll hear them."

"I sleep with one eye open. And the door open. I'll hear them too."

Gray shook his head. "It's not necessary for you to stay awake. I've had years of experience as a ranger keeping my eye on everything."

"I've had a bit of experience myself, Gray. I've slept on a chair watching her door more nights than I want to admit."

"You don't have to do that anymore. Get some rest," he told her, his voice gentle and strong.

Erin rocked back in the chair. "Thank you, Gray. Good night."

"Goodnight, Erin."

He hesitated before she heard the sound of his boots on the stairs. Her husband was turning into a decent man..

Who knew even a week ago that the two of them would be civil towards each other.

*****

Every store in Mill Ridge had bells on the entrance doors. It wasn't because they were a single standard bell that jingled slightly when the door was pushed open. No sir, they were holiday jingle bells made out of heavy brass or metal that was so loud Erin heard the mercantile's bells go off from down the street.

Her mother was clutching onto her arm, more tightly than usual. "Is everything okay, Mother?"

The older woman nodded, but Erin noticed she looked a bit frightened. "Those bells are quite loud. They scared me at first. But, I'm fine. When will we see Frank and Gray again?"

"Soon, Mother. We are meeting at the new café in thirty minutes. Remember we are going to buy some material for our new dresses."

Her mother's eyes lit up. "I am so excited and I can use the sewing machine in the parlor!"

They had this conversation twice this morning. Her mother's memory seemed to be getting worse. Erin was truly worried, but overall her mother was happier than she'd ever been. There was always a smile where before she seemed so sad. It had everything to do with Frank.

As they went inside the mercantile, her mother jumped at the sound of the bells going off. She pulled on Erin's arm harder, until she saw the rolls of material and got distracted. They spent over fifteen minutes choosing material. "I'd also like this material, dear."

"It's gorgeous," Erin told her, but didn't understand why she would want the bright red material. It wasn't something her mother would normally choose.

The elder Mr. Dunleavy was at the store today instead of his son. "Good morning, Mr. Dunleavy. May we have some material cut, please."

"Give me a moment to get there. I'm retired, you know. Except my son was going over to Wichita Falls on the train this morning and asked me to take over."

Erin gave him a smile. "It's nice to have you here."

"Thank you, ma'am. It's nice to be here, but I like to fish more now that I'm not needed here every day."

Erin did notice the older man walked a little slower. It took him longer than she realized to cut and fold the material. He placed the material in a nice cloth bag with handles. "Thank you, Mr. Dunleavy. You have a pleasant day."

"Same to you both," he told them, then promptly sat on a high stool behind the counter. Erin was surprised the old man was so pleasant to her. The last time she had come through Mill Ridge when she worked for the Teacher's Association, he was not too nice. Well, she'd be the first to admit she hadn't been the most pleasant woman in town.

They strolled down the boarded walk, exchanging pleasantries with those passing by. Many of the store fronts were decorated with holly berries and wreaths made from pine trees. The spirit of the holidays was in the air. A buggy with a horse pulling it was decorated with red ribbons. An older woman was driving the buggy and stopped directly in front of the mercantile. She hurried to the front door and walked in, the bells jingling in the distance.

Frank and Gray were standing in front of the church speaking with two men. Both stood as tall as him. When the ladies got to the church, Gray reached out and took Erin's arm. "Gentlemen, this is Erin, my wife."

Both men looked surprised. "Good afternoon, ma'am."

"Good afternoon," the other one said, his voice low and gravelly. He gave her a pleasant smile before turning back to the men.

"Good afternoon," Erin's mother said, her voice high-pitched.

"These two men are my comrades," Gray told the others. "Noah Holloway and Grant Jennings. Grant and I worked together often."

"It's a pleasure to meet you," Erin told him. She tried to let him know without being rude that her mother was getting anxious, but he had it already figured out.

"We must be on our way. Make it a point to visit the farm. We're only ten minutes from town."

Frank took her mother's arm and helped her across the street to Sarah's café. The small building was much different than Evangeline's place down the street. This one was much friendlier than the other and they found an empty table where they could watch the outside world from their spot in front of the big window.

"I was told at one time there was only one place to eat in town. That's before the railroad built tracks from Wichita Falls. Now, there are several cafés and even a fancy restaurant. There's even talk of building an orphanage behind the church," Gray told her.

Three ladies from the next table turned their heads all at once. "There has been a change of plans. That is not going to happen," the youngest of the three mentioned.

"Don't mind her, she's passionate about the orphan children and will speak up if anyone talks about them, " one of the others said with a smile.

"I'm sorry, ma'am. I was just telling my new wife what I heard," Gray retorted. He gave the ladies a smile and Erin wondered if he wasn't flirting. She watched the ladies closely but they didn't seem to be bothered by Gray's charming smile.

The three turned to Erin as the oldest of the three spoke up. "Hello, my name is Nora White Rivers. This is my former neighbor Catherine Young Cooper, and this young lady who interrupted your dining is my daughter-in-law, Naomi White."

They exchanged pleasantries while the men got quiet. Erin had to smile at the fact Gray didn't quite know what to say now that he wasn't the center of attention any longer. "It's a pleasure to meet you, ladies. I live on a farm about ten minutes from town. It would be my pleasure to have you visit." Plus, it would give her mother a chance to converse with others. Ruth seemed to be in her glory, chatting with one of the ladies. It almost seemed as if her memory loss was completely gone.

Erin knew better. She caught Gray watching her, an amused grin on his face until Frank wanted attention and the two conversed quietly at the table. "We'd love to visit. Actually, our ranch isn't that far from here," Nora told Erin. "We are having a Christmas celebration with our staff and neighbors next Saturday. You are all welcome to stop by. It will be early afternoon so everyone can get back home before dark."

"That sounds lovely," Erin told her. She meant those words, which surprised Erin. Mostly, the women of Mill Ridge had been cold towards her because of her terrible attitude. It was her own fault. These ladies didn't know who she was or that she had been horrible to Miss Jennie, the town's teacher. Hopefully, they'd never find out even if Jennie had forgiven her.

"We decided to hold it a week before Christmas since everyone has their own Yuletide plans. It wasn't always like that, but our ranch has grown so much. Now that my neighbor has moved to Cooper's Ridge with her new husband, I try to find any excuse to bring them back to my place."

The two ladies smiled at each other. They seemed to have a genuine friendship. It was nice to watch. Erin wondered if she'd ever have that kind of relationship with another person. For now, her attention had to be with her mother. Everything she did, it was for the woman who brought life to her.

"We'd better get going," the youngest told the two others. "Miss Addie is visiting her boarding house and we promised to stop in for tea."

"Oh, yes. We can't disappoint our dear Miss Addie."

"Goodbye. It was nice to meet all of you." Nora gave each person at the table a smile. "Oh, about the party next Saturday. Be sure to bring a ribbon or some type of decor for the tree. We'll be decorating a huge tree in the yard and everyone brings a decoration. It's our ritual of sorts."

"Oh, why thank you, dear. I'll sew up something especially nice for the tree."

"You sew?" Nora seemed quite interested in Ruth's admission.

"Yes, I do. As long as I can get the mechanical contraption to work, I'll be making my dear daughter a new dress for your party."

"How lovely. I am looking for someone to help with a few projects. I would be happy to come see you next week to discuss this."

"Of course, please do."

The ladies left. Erin's jaw snapped shut when she realized it had been hanging open. Her mother secured a job within ten minutes of meeting Nora White Rivers. Erin didn't see one trace of a confused woman. She was alert and anxious to help her new friend. Amazing. Even Frank seemed intrigued at how Ruth's eyes were so lit up.

Frank gave her mother's arm a squeeze. "You got a job! Now all I need to do is find one and we can build our own farm!"

Erin glanced at Gray but he was too busy staring at his uncle. "You don't have to get a job, Uncle Frank. Remember you live with me and we take care of you."

Erin interrupted before Frank got too angry at his nephew's words. "Frank, what Gray meant was you work for him on the farm. He pays you by giving you a roof over your head and feeds you. He also brings you here to this lovely café. Isn't that nice/"

Frank nodded and his upper body moved slowly back and forth."I forgot. I'm sorry. Sometimes I can't remember who I am. Isn't that just plain silly?" His eyes got huge and he stared at her waiting for an answer.

"It isn't silly at all to be forgetful. I believe it is a natural occurrence. Don't worry, Frank."

"Yes, listen to my servant. She does know a lot."

Erin sighed. Gray caught her eye, giving his head a slight shake as if to tell her not to get upset.

As they were leaving the café, Gray reached out and took her hand, placing it in his own. He gave her a gentle squeeze. "It's going to all work out."

"I hope so," she admitted, knowing Gray knew all too well how frustrated she was feeling.

"The holidays are here. Your mother will be busy sewing and I'll keep Frank occupied at the farm."

Erin looked up into his face. Gray was a handsome man, even with a patch over one eye. "Do you ever miss being a ranger?"

He frowned. "What made you ask?"

She shrugged. "I don't know. Taking care of your uncle must be a far cry from the exciting work of a Texas Ranger."

He grunted. "It's far from exciting, Erin."

She tilted her head to stare at him. "I can't imagine. It has to be more exciting than working on a farm all day, following Frank around to make sure he doesn't get into trouble."

Gray shook his head. "There's where you are wrong. There are many nights alone while on an outlaws trail. Months of hiding in the shadows as a matter of fact. It gets lonely. This farm is the most exciting thing to happen to me in a long time. I don't regret leaving the rangers one bit. Besides, I was ready to settle down. I just got luckier than most."

Lucky! What was that supposed to mean? And what did he mean by he was ready to settle down? Had this whole situation of marrying her cause him to give up a future he had wanted with someone else? Erin was always blunt, causing her to be disliked by many. But, she had to know if he was interested in someone else. "I'm sorry if this situation caused you to change plans with someone. I -"

Gray stopped her. "Did you think I had a woman in the background? Oh, Erin. No. I didn't and I wouldn't marry someone else if I were in love already. That's a fools game."

Relief tugged at her heartstrings. "I'm glad."

He gave her a pleasing look. "You are?"

She nodded.

"Good. Because I am, too."

Chapter 8

"Oh! My! Mama, you are a miracle worker!"

Her mother sat at the wooden contraption smiling up at Erin as she twirled across the room. "This is the prettiest dress I've ever had." Erin danced in front of the long mirror Frank had carried down from the upstairs bedroom. The folks who owned the place had left so much behind.

The extra bedroom had served as a storage area with a plethora of trunks and furniture to choose from. It was odd to leave so much behind that Erin wondered about the people who lived here before Gray bought the property. Perhaps next time she was in town, she'd question Nester Cravell.

"I see a flaw. Come here, Erin."

Her mother quickly spotted a hole she missed and helped Erin out of the dress so she could fix it. Her mother sewed up the flaw and handed the dress back.

Erin held the dress close. "I am in love with this dress. Thank you, Mother."

"You will be the prettiest woman at the party."

Erin frowned. "Do you think it's too fancy? After all, we're going to a ranch. The party is for the workers and family."

Her mother made it a point to think about what Erin said by placing her finger in the center of her chin, then shook her head. "Not at all. Why, daughter, you should never be afraid to show your beauty."

Erin wanted to tell her that she was the one who always told her to hide her beauty, that was one of the reasons her father had protected her and died. But that was a long time ago. Her mother wouldn't remember those days. It was time to leave the past right where it was. "I better go get ready. We'll be leaving in another hour."

She hurried to her room, where a warm basin and pitcher waited. After washing up, Erin placed the gorgeous red material over her head and proceeded to close the long row of buttons her mother had sewn up the front. The dress was completely different than the clothes she'd been wearing the last few years.

Actually, Erin realized she missed wearing pretty things. For the last few years, she had covered herself with dull, ugly brown material. She peeked at her reflection in the wall mirror above her dresser.

And stared.

She didn't look like the same person. Her mother had put her hair up in pins earlier, letting a few of the soft curls loosely fall around her face. There was a red ribbon running through her hair to match the dress. Erin slipped into her black kid boots, knowing a pair of slippers would not work where they were going.

It didn't matter that the boots were cleaned to perfection. They were worn and it showed. Luckily, her mother thought of everything and made the hem long enough to hide the boots. She slid a drawer open from her jewelry box and stared at the garnet necklace her father had given her. It had been his mother's necklace and the day she turned sixteen, he gave her this gift. Erin had hid it away all this time. It was time to show it off.

The clasps were stiff, but she snapped them closed and stared at her reflection in the mirror. The rich, deep scarlet stones twinkled against her pale skin. It looked perfect hanging just below her collarbone. Erin sighed. She felt like a princess.

The color of her dress matched the stones. Erin wondered if her mother had chosen the material knowing she'd wear her garnet jewelry. How was it that her mother remembered such small details and yet forgot where she was going or who her own daughter was at times?

It was all a mystery she wanted to put behind her for just one day. She placed a small hat over her hair and tilted it forward. Erin leaned in, giving the girl in the mirror a smile that lit up her face. She giggled. No one would know she was the former prim and proper Teacher's Association employee.

She heard the men come down from upstairs where they had been getting dressed and then her mother was calling out to her. "Come along, dear. We don't want to be late."

Erin exited her room. She took two steps into the kitchen and stopped, almost afraid to reveal herself. Gray's back was facing her as he leaned down to make sure the stove was cooled off. He straightened up, turned around to say something to Frank when he stopped in his tracks.

She didn't know he held a glass of liquid in his hand until it dropped to the floor, causing a splash against the bottom of his pant legs.

He stared. His mouth opened and closed. Then, he stared at her harder, ignoring the fact he made a mess on the floor and her mother was trying to find the mop to clean it up. Frank was shaking his hand at Ruth, who was on a mission to find the mop.

No, he ignored all of it as he stared right into her very soul. Erin stood helpless. She was afraid to move. He was watching her like a hawk ready to pounce on a field mouse.

She worried he'd laugh at her all dressed up and fancy. But he wasn't laughing. No, he was giving her that look that made her feel as if she were about to be taken in his arms and kissed thoroughly.

Then, he turned away and she wanted to run and hide. She had thought he was pleased until he turned away like she burnt him with hot steaming water. Was she a failure at everything she did?

*****

The glass slid from his hand without any thought that it would crash to the floor scattering pieces of glass everywhere. When he turned to find Erin in a beautiful, red gown with her hair softly falling around her beautiful face, it took him by surprise. He forgot his uncle stood beside him, or her mother was making a commotion about the accident. He heard the two arguing about a broom, but Gray didn't care.

All he wanted was to pull Erin into his arms and kiss her like she'd never been kissed before. The desire was so strong, he almost took a step towards her until he forced himself to turn away. How the hell did he wind up like this? His wife stood there looking so beautiful and yet he didn't want to scare her away.

He remembered her story about the last time she went to a ball the night her father killed a man and he knew this was a huge step for her today. Gray wasn't going to let her relive the past, but make new memories for her to replace them with. And that wasn't by kissing her like a madman! Even if he wanted to.

He growled at himself, detesting the fact he was no longer a whole man. The damn eye patch was ugly. She wouldn't want to kiss a man like him anyway. He knew it. He began to question everything he said and did. Each emotion he went through worked on his nerves. Angry at himself more than anything, Gray mumbled something to his uncle and went outside to bring the horse and wagon from the barn. He needed air. Lots of air.

Frank followed. "Are you ill, son? What was that all about?"

"I lost my footing and slipped, Uncle Frank."

"I was watching the whole thing and you didn't slip, son. Maybe the young lady was too much for you to take in. It sure scared the devil out of you!"

Which made Gray fume even more. If Frank noticed, that meant Erin may have too and he didn't want her to know how desperately he wanted her. There was no way he'd scare her like that other man did. Gray ran a hand through his hair. "I guess you are right, Uncle Frank."

"Ruth sure did a good job with her dress."

"Yes, she did." When he saw his wife standing in the doorway, he had to admit it shocked him. He knew she was beautiful but she hid it behind frumpy clothes and pulled back hair. The plain loose gowns she always wore hid her beauty.

The gown was a velvety red with a tight bodice that was much lower than her other dresses. The material was tight around her waist until it flounced out and fell in layers to the floor. She had an antique necklace that laid against the pearl white of her skin. He wanted to place tiny kisses there and had to restrain himself from gathering her in his arms and doing so.

It was going to be a long night.

The ladies were waiting on the porch when the two men brought the wagon up. He jumped from the driver's seat and held out his hand for his wife. She glanced shyly and took his hand, giving him a sad smile. Almost as if she had to tolerate his help.

What had happened? "Erin, did I upset you when I dropped the glass?"

She nodded. "Very much so."

"I'm sorry. I'll buy you more."

She glanced at him and shook her head. "It had nothing to do with the glass." He wanted to say more, but her mother interrupted.

"Why do I have to sit back here with the help? Shouldn't she go in the back of the wagon?" Ruth was having a moment.

"No, Mother. I will not sit in the back of the wagon. I'm your daughter and will sit with you on the back bench."

"You are? Why didn't someone tell me? Well, then, dear. I think it is fine for you to sit with me. What a lovely dress you are wearing."

Gray got up front and began their trek to the ranch, wondering what it would be like to dance with Erin. He'd never know because the last thing he wanted to do was upset her.

*****

Erin sighed. She glanced at the two men sitting up front on the bench and scooted closer to her mother. It was going to be a bumpy ride. She hoped and prayed her mother would be back to normal by the time they got to the White-Rivers Ranch.

The ride lasted almost an hour and fifteen minutes, but it was easily found when they turned the wagon down a long lane. A huge barn stood in the way of the road, but when they went down the lane, it opened up to see an orchard, a few houses along the landscape and a huge two-story house near the barn. A few other buildings were dotted against the ranch and a road that led to a fence was in the far distance.

"This is quite huge," her mother whispered. That's when Erin wondered if it made her nervous being around such a large group of strangers.

Erin leaned over and patted her hand. "If you get frightened or anxious, Mother, let any of us know and we will be on our way."

Ruth waved her off. "Oh, I won't get anxious or nervous. I'm used to a lot of people." Even though she said it with confidence, Erin lifted her face to the clouds and whispered a tiny prayer to the man up above. *Please, Lord, let this party go smoothly and keep mother and Frank safe.*

Erin felt better knowing the two were in God's hands. Although, the elders were placed in her and Gray's hands, ultimately. They were responsible for keeping the two from danger, but a little godly intervention never hurt as far as she was concerned.

Frank and Gray stepped down from the wagon, offering a hand to the ladies. Ruth giggled while Erin tried to avoid Gray's gaze. The thought that he may not want to escort her the way she looked bothered her to no end. Erin thought she looked beautiful but Gray had dropped that glass in shock and turned away after. What was she to think?

"Welcome! Welcome!" Nora came toward them, with a man dressed like a cowboy with bright red hair. He took off his wide-brimmed hat and nodded to the ladies before shaking hands with the men. "Ladies, if you'll come with me, I want you to meet my sons and their wives. And my grandchildren of course."

Nora was a fast walker. Even in her lovely party dress, it was hard to keep up with her. Ruth pulled Erin's arm, tugged at her. "Keep up, Erin! Stop poking around," she whispered as if Erin were a child.

They stopped at a long table where others were gathered, laughing and talking, along with small children and some babies in laps.

"This is my clan," Nora said, laughing. "Rusty, my husband just nudged me so I forgot to say it's his clan, too."

Rusty tipped the brim of his hat. "Thank you, darling. Now how about we let these good folks sit awhile and enjoy the party after you introduce them to every single member of our family." Rusty looked at the men and rolled his eyes.

"I've got quite the collection of fine horses in the barn if you men want to see them," he told Gray.

"We're coming with!"

Three of the men at the table stood.

Nora quickly introduced them as if she knew they were going to run off. "Those are my boys, Luke, Adam and Samuel. Then, the two that are sneaking up behind them are Catherine's boys, Russell and Wesley and I want to apologize for what is about to happen."

As Gray and Frank followed Rusty to the barn, the men behind went running towards the doors of the big building. But, before they got there, the last two ran up behind them and they all tumbled down wrestling each other. Most of the other guests were laughing and making comments.

Erin watched, amused at their antics. Why would a bunch of grown men act like little boys?

One of the women stood up and turned to Erin. "I'm sure you are wondering why they act like that? We will never understand them. Hello, I am Samuel's wife, Callie, and the rest of us here are all married to those wild, crazy men!"

Erin was introduced to the other women. She was surprised they smiled and made her feel welcome. It was the first time since she'd been in Mill Ridge anyone seemed to give her attention. There were babies everywhere it seemed. Ruth sat on one of the benches holding one of the infants. She was content to rock the baby so Erin didn't feel as if she had to stand on top of her. She moved around the yard, speaking to the others.

She was glad the women had dressed in fine gowns, too. At first, Erin thought the dress her mother made was too fancy for the party, but now that she saw the others, she fit right in. Her red dress didn't stand out like she thought it would.

Nora stood in the center of the yard, striking a bell. The sound caught everyone's attention. "I want to thank you all for coming to our Christmas party. There is plenty of food for everyone to enjoy. I'd like to welcome our new residents, Mr. and Mrs. Gray Randall. Also, Gray's uncle, Frank and Mrs. Randall's mother, Ruth. Please be sure to give them a warm welcome."

Everyone clapped. While Nora introduced a few others attending, Erin blushed at all the attention. Even Ruth looked up and gave the hostess a quirky smile. Erin was so glad to be here. Now if only Gray would pay attention to her, but he hurried to the barn along with the other men. She hoped he wasn't wrestling in the hay. The thought made her giggle.

"What's so funny?" The voice was so close it made Erin jump. She cried out, causing a few others in the vicinity to stare. When she smiled, they returned her smile before turning away.

"Gray Randall, you scared the daylights out of me. I thought you were in the barn with the others."

The fiddle struck up a fast tune that changed the atmosphere of the party. Everyone spread in a large circle and the dancing began.

"I was until the music began. Would you care to dance?" Gray asked, holding out his hand.

Erin gave him a stern look. "Only if you promise not to scare me again."

He leaned in. "I promise."

She took his outstretched hand and followed him to the center of the dance area. The musicians were in a half-circle while some children and adults were dancing and others watched. She swung around and found herself in his arms.

They danced and laughed, enjoying the melodic festivities. When the music slowed, he gathered her in his arms and pulled her a tiny bit closer. "This is nice," he mentioned.

She agreed. "I'm glad we came, Gray."

"So am I." Before she realized what was happening, he dipped his head and kissed her gently on the mouth. She didn't try to turn away or even feel embarrassed that so many others surrounded them. It seemed right and felt just wonderful, after all, Gray was her husband.

He pulled away and stared into her soul. Actually, it was her eyes but she felt as if he knew everything there was to know about her from the look he gave her. She gave him a warm smile and lifted her hand, letting her fingers gently run over his eye patch. "What happened to your eye, Gray?"

He shrugged. "War injury, you could say. It's all part of being a Texas Ranger." Even though he didn't seem to want to talk about it, he allowed her touch to continue. She sighed when a small child tugged on her skirt. She looked down to find a beautiful blonde-haired child there.

Erin let go of her husband and leaned down as best as she could. "Do you want to tell me something?"

The little girl nodded, clasping her hands together in a nervous gesture. "Your mommy said to tell you-"

Chapter 9

Erin became worried. "Tell me what?" she asked, gently, seeing the girl was having a hard time getting out the words.

"Your mommy went to the pasture to ride a horse. She told me to tell you that she was going to ride the pony. My grandmother doesn't let people ride the horses."

Erin stood. "Is your grandmother's name Nora?"

The little face looked blank. "I don't know! She lives right there!" The girl pointed to Nora's house.

"Thank you. I'll go fetch my mommy now. You've been a big helper."

Erin turned away and grabbed Gray's hand. He hadn't heard everything the child said. "Where is Frank?"

Gray strode along, confused. "He was talking to the men over there before we danced. I told him to stay with them." Gray headed towards the men in front of the barn. "Did you see my uncle?"

"The older man you came here with?" Luke asked.

"That's right. He gets forgetful at times."

"His wife came and took him to see the horses in the coral. I'm sure they're fine."

Gray nodded and headed towards the coral, taking charge.

Erin wasn't sure if Gray heard what the child told her. "The little girl said my mother was going to ride a horse."

"Let's hope it isn't too late!" Gray walked faster, pulling her along. She called out for her mother, but the noise from the party in general was too loud. Her mother would never hear her.

They turned the corner to see a body lying still on the ground. Three horses were dancing nervously from the other side of the coral, staying far from the two inside. Frank was bending over her mother.

Erin's heart leapt to her throat. She let go of Gray's hand and ran to the gate, opening it without a hitch. She knew Gray followed behind so she didn't bother to close the gate. In the background, she heard the gate latch but didn't bother to make sure.

"Mother? Mother?" She called her name over and over until she got to the still form. Erin knelt down, the skirt of her red dress on the dirt but that was the last thing on her mind.

Frank had a hold of his wife's hand. "Come on now, Ruth. Stop fooling around. We have to get back home before dark. Ruth? Do you hear me, Ruth?"

When Erin got there, Frank looked up at her like he was lost. Truly lost and not from his forgetfulness. He truly loved his wife. It crossed Erin's mind that if her mother didn't make it, the loss would crush Frank.

Erin felt her mother's brow. She was warm and there was a trickle of sweat along her brow. She ran the palm of her hand over her mother's cheek. "Wake up, Mother. It's time to go home."

Ruth's eyes opened up wide. "Well, why didn't you say so. I am ready to go home and get in my own bed. This one is not comfortable at all. Don't tell the hostess. She would be upset and she's a lovely woman."

Erin was not going to try to explain to her mother that she was lying in the middle of a horse corral. "Let's get you up."

Frank took his wife's arm, but Gray moved in and lifted her mother to her feet. Frank took over from there, placing kisses on her cheek. "Oh, lovey, you scared me. I thought you were going to die."

"Die? Whatever are you talking about, Frank? I was taking a nap!"

Frank shook his head. "I'm afraid not, dear. You fell off a horse. I know because I saw you fall. Scared the living daylights out of me, too." He looked at his nephew. "I swear to you she did."

Grant patted his uncle on the shoulder. "It's fine, Uncle Frank. We better get back."

Ruth gasped when she tried to walk. "Oh, my foot!" It took two strides for Gray to pick up Ruth and carry her to the wagon, where he placed her on the back bench. Frank got up beside her and began to check her other limbs to make sure she hadn't hurt anything else.

Nora and her neighbor, Catherine, hurried to Erin's side. "Is everything all right?"

"It's fine. My mother gets forgetful at times. Your granddaughter told me she wanted to ride a horse and we found her on the ground in the coral. Mother claims she was taking a nap, but Frank, who is also forgetful, said she fell."

"Oh, dear, I'm so sorry. What can we do to help you?"

Gray interrupted. "We'll be on our way, ma'am. Thank you for the invitation. It was a very nice party."

"It was a pleasure. Will you allow me to send for a doctor for your mother? I saw you carrying her to the wagon. Is she hurt?"

Erin shook her head. "It's her ankle. We'll get her back to the farm and if we need to, we are only ten minutes from town. Gray can go for Doc Hart if there is a need. I do have some herbs and medicine at home."

Home. It sounded nice. Erin didn't think she'd ever have a place to live where others cared so much. But, here in Mill Ridge and beyond she realized how much people did care. Gray helped her onto the wagon. She had to sit in the front seat beside him since Frank was catering to his wife in the back seat.

"Good-bye, Nora. Thank you for the wonderful time. It was a pleasure to meet you, Catherine."

"Lovely to meet you as well, Erin. Someone said you were with the Teacher's Association?"

Erin almost denied it since she didn't want anyone to remember what a prude she had been. She gave Catherine a smile. "It's been quite some time since leaving their employ."

"Hopefully, you still remember how things work. I live in Cooper's Ridge and want to start a school. We are adopting some orphan children and they will need to go to school. Right now, the only folks who live there are reformed outlaws and some women who help to run the shops. As soon as we find more families who want to adopt orphans, I'd love for you to come help us set up a school if you would."

Erin was so relieved that no one spoke to her about her awful past behavior. "I'd be delighted. Please, let me know. Perhaps, Gray and I can come visit Cooper's Ridge."

Catherine waved. "Please do." She stepped closer to the wagon. "It does get quite lonely there at times. That's when I come visit Nora and the ladies here. Until we fill up the place with families, that is."

"If I can be of service, I'd consider it an honor." Erin waved. How wonderful to be asked for advice on starting a school. She would make sure to visit Cooper's Ridge as soon as she was able. It brought a smile to her face. She loved being on the farm, but she also loved working to better other's lives as well.

Her husband looked furious. Gray didn't say much the whole way back to the farm. Once there, he lifted her mother while Erin went inside to turn on the oil lamps. It was almost dusk, so she went through each room to make sure there was plenty of light.

Gray laid her mother on her bed while Erin poured water. Frank stood by her, cooing and speaking soft words. Erin thought it was endearing and yet knew beyond a shadow of a doubt Frank was unable to take care of his wife. Which made Erin and Gray's job even harder.

Erin took a bowl filled with water and set it on the nightstand. She peeled off her mother's slipper and pressed around her foot. There didn't seem to be much swelling at all. Actually, there was no swelling. "Mother, how does your foot feel?"

Ruth gave her a sweet smile. "My foot is fine. Why are you meddling at my feet? I'm just tired."

"Mother, do you remember falling from the horse?"

Ruth laughed out loud. "I had a fall from a horse? You are kidding, right, dear? I never got a chance to get up on the saddle. Darn horse took off and I dropped to the ground. Then I thought, well, while I'm down here I may as well take a nap since there was so much going on at the party. It felt good, too. Too bad we had to leave right away. Now, I'm wide awake."

"Now, now, my love. I'll make you a cup of tea and we'll sit and talk."

Ruth gazed at her husband." If I get tired of talking, will you read me a book?"

"I'd love to read to you, my love. Now, excuse me while I make some tea."

"I'll help," Gray told her. They both nodded, knowing there was no way they would allow Frank alone in the kitchen.

An hour later, after Ruth finally fell asleep to the sound of Frank's voice as he read to her, Frank yawned and fell promptly to sleep as well. He was sitting in the chair when Erin went in to find snoring noises renting the air. She helped Frank get settled in, dousing the lamp and leaving their door open slightly.

Erin made her way to the stove where a fire burned, keeping a pot of hot water warm. A lone cup sat on the counter so she picked it up and poured hot water into it while finding some tea. After allowing it to stew for a few minutes, she carried the cup out to the porch, somehow knowing Gray would be there, also. He had been the one to keep the water warm and leave the cup on the stove for her.

She sat beside him on the bench and leaned back. "It's been quite a day, hasn't it?"

Gray nodded. "It sure has. Erin?" He turned to her. "I don't think this is going to get any better. I understand if you want to high-tail it out of here as fast as you can."

Erin shook her head. "Why in the world would you think I'd want to leave?"

He took a slug from his cup. "I don't know why you'd want to stay. Who wants to stay married to a one-eyed man who is no good for anyone?"

She turned in her seat. "Gray? Am I hearing you right? You are a wonderful man! The thought that you would give up a lucrative career to take care of your uncle shows me the extent of the person inside of you."

He reached over and gently took her hand. "Thank you, Erin. I say the same for you as well."

"I have no choice. She is my mother. Is there really any other way?"

"I'm afraid there is, Erin. It's a big, cold world out there and the things people do to each other can be terrible." He leaned forward.

"You could have kept working and placed your mother in an insane asylum."

"That's a horrible thing to do!"

He agreed. "And yet so many people do that to their family members."

"Not me. I'd never send her away. No matter how much she hurt me in the past. She's my mother and family helps each other, no matter what."

"I feel the same way, Erin." He gave her hand a squeeze.

She looked him in the face. "Then why would you think just because you have a patch over your eye you are less of a man? Or, that I would not want you?"

He shrugged and looked away, staring at the darkness of the night. "I don't know, Erin. We didn't start off well at all. I figured you thought I was flawed. Truth is I'm ashamed of my physical appearance."

She giggled.

He turned to stare at her. "There you go, giggling again. How can you think this is funny?"

"I do that when I'm nervous." She stood up and went to his side. Taking both his hands, she stared him in the eye. Then, she let one go, took her hand and lifted the patch. "No, don't pull away," she ordered when she felt him tense.

Erin leaned in and gently brushed her lips over his damaged eye. "I will never judge you because of this flaw. It is a badge of courage you wear, my sweet Gray." She kissed his eye again and then replaced the patch.

He sat there, so quiet it worried her that she had overstepped her boundaries. But she had to make him understand that if they were to make this marriage work, he had to believe that she didn't care how he looked. And she didn't. "You look rather dangerous and like a man who won't stand still for any nonsense. Maybe someday you will tell me the story of how it happened. Goodnight, Gray."

Erin let go of his hand, turned and went inside quickly. She closed her eyes when she got to the safety of her bedroom and let out a long sigh. Would he think of her as a trollop with her forward ways? Or, would he realize that she cared about him more than she dreamed she'd ever care about a man?

She took off her beautiful dress and hung it carefully on the hook on the wall beside her door, replacing it with a dressing gown. Realizing her pitcher of water was empty, Erin had to go out to the pump that sat right off the porch to refill. She didn't like to leave her room in her bedclothes, but she had a ritual of washing her face that prompted her to do so. Being away from home all day, she had forgotten to replenish her water supply.

She hadn't heard Gray come inside, so she figured he was still outside, which made it a bit more tricky to go out in her night robe. But they were married and she was covered up. He'd just have to get used to her like this. She needed water!

Before she lifted the handle to pump water, an arm shot out, taking the pitcher from her hand. "Let me do that for you," Gray offered, taking over her chore as she stepped back.

"Thank you," She told him, watching him while he pumped the water and filled her pitcher. He splashed some over the top and she smiled.

"This is heavy, I'll carry it inside for you."

"Seriously, Gray, I am able to carry my own water."

"You are my wife and I want to do this for you."

"Fine." She followed him inside, and stepped to the side as he set the water pitcher beside the bowl on her dresser.

He took a few steps backward, then swung around and came at her like a tornado across a Kansas prairie. She lifted her arms and welcomed him. Gray cupped her face with her hands and thoroughly kissed her. Erin was out of breath when he finally pulled away.

Then he lifted her up and began to carry her across the kitchen floor and through the parlor. "What are you doing?"

He turned to go up the stairs to his room. He stopped midway up the steps. "Tell me now if you don't want to come to my room."

She didn't hesitate. "I do."

"So be it." He carried her the rest of the way and kicked the door shut. Erin didn't have time to speculate on anything at that moment because Gray was kissing her again.

Chapter 10

A Week later - 2 days before Christmas Eve

"Mother, we are going to Mill Ridge to help sing Christmas carols. Frank and Gray will be driving us there and we will be walking around with the ladies and children while they have a meeting at the sheriff's office. Then, they'll meet up with us at the church for hot cocoa and baked goods."

"That sounds lovely. Why are you wearing that old brown gown again?"

Erin shrugged. "I don't know, mother. I suppose everyone in Mill Ridge has seen me like this for so long, I just put it on this morning."

Ruth shook her head. "That won't do at all, dear. You must wear the red one again."

"No, Mother. Not today."

"Then, perhaps you'll wear this." Gray came into the kitchen where they were having a cup of tea together. He handed her a package wrapped in newspaper. She had to smile at the makeshift twine tied in a bow.

"A gift? For me? It's not Christmas morning yet."

"This is special. Go ahead, open it."

She tore open the package to find a long, full-length coat with a five-layered cape collar. It was luxurious compared to the other one her mother had previously placed in the stove. "I can't accept this. Where did you get such a luxury, Gray?" She knew he didn't have much money left after buying the farm. Actually, she wanted to tell him about her savings and still hadn't. Earlier, she had wanted to keep quiet about her savings, but now that they were truly married, she knew it was the right thing to do to tell him about her account.

"Your mother made it. I bought the material at a shop in town."

Erin swung around. "Mother, what a wonderful gift. How in the world did you hide this from me?"

"I have my ways, my dear."

She gave Ruth a hug and then rose up on her toes. She placed a kiss on Gray's mouth, along with a shy smile. "Thank you," she whispered. "Give me a moment."

Erin hurried off to her bedroom, getting rid of the drab brown dress she wore and replacing it with the red one her mother made her that she wore to the party. After she changed, she buttoned her coat and added a matching hat. She covered her hair that was slightly pulled back with a red ribbon to match the dress underneath.

Gray whistled. Frank followed suit and tried to whistle, too. He failed, but it didn't deter him. "You look wonderful, young lady," Frank told her.

The mood was jolly as they headed into town in the wagon. Erin was so excited to show the folks at Mill Ridge how much she had changed. Maybe they'd forgive her for all of her mean words she'd spoken to many others before. Miss Jennie had forgiven her when she first came to town. Hopefully, the rest would as well.

Then she looked over at Gray and realized it didn't matter if they thought she was a horrible person. All that mattered was her new thrown-together family. Her mother had never been so happy with Frank by her side. She may forget things and had a rough start, but with the care of Erin and Gray, along with Frank trying to care for her, Ruth had settled down nicely. Frank on the other hand, followed Gray everywhere, like a lost puppy. At times she knew it drove her husband crazy, but he'd ride off some evenings and come back an hour later refreshed.

It was all they could do to keep going this way. Taking care of two elders with this morosis diagnosis was terribly hard. But, determination and frustration worked hand in hand. Erin and Gray both knew that at some point, they would have to watch their loved ones die.

She shook her head, not wanting to think about the end.

"Is everything all right, dear? You have such a perplexed look on your face."

Erin reached over and gave her mother a smile. "I'm fine Mother. I love you."

Ruth patted her hand. "I'm glad, dear. I love you, too."

It was then that Erin realized her mother hadn't called her a servant for some time now. Maybe that was a good sign. Perhaps this arrangement was good for all of them in more ways than one.

Gray happened to turn his head and look at her. He gave her a wink with his good eye, making Erin blush. How had she ever thought he was an arrogant, selfish man? In the last few weeks, she saw an honorable, kind hearted man who made sure every one of them were taken care of.

She wondered why he hadn't hired anyone to help with the chores. There was so much to do on a farm. She had offered to help, but it was hard trying to find a way to go outside while her mother was inside sewing away. The older woman always seemed to know just when Erin went outside. Even if it was only for twenty minutes, by the time Erin returned, her mother had gotten into something.

So Erin made it a point not to go outside when her mother was busy inside sewing away. She'd work in the kitchen because that seemed to be where her mother got into trouble. Once Erin found the sugar and flour mixed together. She knew better than to ask why because there was no reasoning to the things Ruth did.

Gray said he understood, but many nights he'd be so exhausted by the time he came inside for supper. Frank was there to help him, but Erin knew that Gray had to chase after him quite often. Most nights they both went to their own beds, exhausted.

After tonight, Erin was going to tell him about her money in the bank and insist he hire someone to help on the farm. Perhaps there was a young fellow who needed the money. She had a good eye so it would not be too difficult to spot a family in need of extra money.

The town of Mill Ridge was bustling with folks everywhere. Women, men and children were heading towards the church where everyone was supposed to gather. Someone had been busy putting up wreaths along the boarded walk. Pine branches were covering rails along the shops in town, along with colorful ornaments that hung from the garnishes. The holiday tension was in the air.

A large group of ladies were already singing as they headed towards the church. It made Erin smile. She hoped her new dress and coat would make her seem more presentable to the ladies here. But, if it didn't, that was all right, too. She had her family and right now, it was all that really mattered.

Gray parked the wagon on the far side of the sheriff's office and helped her down. Frank took care of Ruth and the four of them made their way to the church where almost everyone in town was gathered.

"Frank and I will be back shortly. I want to let the sheriff know we are here, just in case he needs me for anything." Frank followed his nephew as the two made their way across the street. Erin smiled at Gray, realizing that even though he was no longer a ranger, he felt the need to check in with the sheriff as if he were still on duty.

"Who in the world are we going to sing to?" Erin wondered out loud. "It looks like everyone is here."

One of the ladies close to her shook her head. "Hello. I'm Marion Swaggert. There are many elders at home who are not able to come here. Doc Hart and his wife, Caroline, have set up more chairs on the porch at the doctor's office so some of his patients can enjoy the carols. They took their wagon and fetched them from neighboring farms."

"That's very kind of them," Erin said, smiling at the woman. "I'm Erin Randall and this is my mother, Ruth."

"Nice to meet you both. I've heard all about your misfortune. I'm so sorry you had such a rough time in Memphis."

"Whatever do you mean?" Erin's jaw stiffened. She was getting more furious by the moment. The only person that knew anything about her time in Memphis was her husband. Had he told others? It was so hard to believe he'd betray her like that. As she looked around, others tilted their heads and waved, but when she looked into their eyes she saw only pity.

Pity! This was absurd! How did they know what happened? She bent her head and whispered in her mother's ear. "Mother, did you ever mention what happened in Memphis at the Langley Ball with anyone here?"

Her mother looked perplexed. She rose up on her toes and whispered in Erin's ear. "Of course not! Didn't we run from all of that when we left Memphis?"

Erin blushed. Her mother's voice was so loud several people turned to look at them. Now more people were listening. She wanted to be normal but now that everyone in town knew about the incident in Memphis, their lives would be changed once again. They would get stares from everyone because of that incident and it didn't matter if it was pity or not, Erin was ashamed of what happened so long ago.

She wanted to shrink from sight and make a run for home. Except Frank and Gray were coming towards them as if nothing had happened.

"Erin! Ruth! Here we are," Frank called out. The crowd was disbursing into two groups. The ladies who had been singing earlier began a sweet rendition of Silent Night. Ruth took Frank's arm and they followed the rest of the crowd.

Gray held his arm out, but Erin didn't take it. She turned on him like a coyote trapped by a bear. "What did you do?" she accused him, not giving him time to respond. "I trusted you. I was even starting to care deeply and you betrayed me. How could you?"

The look of confusion on Gray's face gave her pause. He almost behaved as if he didn't know what she was talking about. But, he did, he had to! He was the only one who knew! The thought of his betrayal moved her. She walked up to him and lifted her hand.

"What in the -"

Erin slapped him across the face. Gray stood frowning. "I didn't deserve that! What are you doing!"

She knew he could take her over his knee if he was inclined to but she was far too angry at him. "You can go after the folks. I'm taking a much needed break! Stay away from me, Gray! I don't know that I'll ever speak to you again!"

"Erin! Honestly, I do not know what I did wrong!" He kept an eye on Frank and Ruth who were at the back of the crowd getting further away. "I have to go after them."

"Go on then. I'll be walking by myself! How dare you tell everyone what happened in Memphis! I thought I could trust you."

Gray growled. "You can trust me. I never said one word. We'll talk later." He took off after the two elders when they started moving away from the singing crowd. Erin watched as he marched to them and steered them back. He looked back at her, his face angry and determined.

She didn't know what to think. If he hadn't said anything, then who did? And why did she care anymore. That part of her life was over. Wasn't it? Or, was she trying to keep it alive. Was she going to live with the guilt of her father's arrest and the death of the Langley man the rest of her life?

Erin began to walk along the boarded walk, behind the rest of the crowd going in the opposite direction of her family. She just wanted to be alone and think. The words wouldn't come from her mouth. She couldn't sing, nor did she want to. Several ladies smiled and waved to her while holding candles and singing carols.

She reverted to the old Erin, frowning, not giving them the time of day. Until a beautiful woman fell into step beside her. "I heard what you said to your husband," she told Erin, smiling.

What was wrong with this town? Everyone minded her business! She stopped and turned. "Why are you interfering in my affairs?"

The woman continued to smile. "Because it is what I do the best and I'm good at it, too. Did you know I almost got hired by the Chicago Tribune? And, the New York times wanted me as well but I refused because I love my life here. Hello, I'm Charity Ashwood. My husband, Daniel and I own the newspaper in Wichita Falls. I'm sure you've heard of the Wichita Falls Tribune?"

Erin nodded. Of course she had heard of the newspaper. What did this woman want with Erin? "I want you to go away."

"I will if you insist, but I overheard what you said to your husband. Oh, dear, one moment please." Charity cupped her hands around her mouth and whistled. "Daniel, here I am. I'll be right over."

Erin swung around to see a man in a long coat holding a little child in his arms and holding the hand of another one beside him. Her husband nodded and walked on the outskirts of the crowd, keeping up with Charity's movements. "I believe you are wanted," she told Charity.

"My husband knows when I am in the middle of something, he stands back until I'm finished. He's a newspaperman, too, and understands my need as a reporter to get a story."

The whole time she was talking, Charity smiled as if she were telling Erin wonderful news. "I'm sorry, but I don't know why you are following me."

"It's because you are blaming the wrong person. I don't like to interfere in other couples' lives, but, oh, who am I kidding! I know almost everything that goes on and I have to speak up. That was not your husband who told me about the incident. It was the man standing on Doc Hart's porch. See the man leaning against the post?"

It was late afternoon so the sun had gone down a long time ago. The shadows on the porch kept his face hidden. Who was he?

"Did he give you a name?"

"Langley, like the fellow who died by your father's hand."

"I'd appreciate it if you toned that down a little. I hate the reminder."

"I'm sorry, Mrs. Randall. I get overly excited about things. When I see a wrong, I like to make it right. I better get to my family.

You were blaming the wrong man. Go find your husband and tell him. It will be worth it, dear."

With those words, just as she had pounced on Erin, the woman reporter disappeared into the crowd.

Erin slowed her steps. She didn't know why a stranger would reveal her story. She left Memphis so no one would ever needle them about it again. Now, someone was here, telling the whole town her business.

Charity was right. She turned and hurried towards the other crowd of carolers, wanting to get to her husband. Maybe she should go to the sheriff instead, but realized her husband was well trained in the law. He'd get to the bottom of this!

Plus, she had to ask his forgiveness. The look on his face when she walked away had touched her heartstrings something fierce. Knowing now how she accused him falsely made her feel ashamed.

A hand on her arm stopped Erin in her tracks. She swung around to face the man who had been standing on the doctor's porch. He wore a heavy long coat that hung to his knees. It was way too warm for Texas weather. A wide-brimmed hat covered his hair and part of his face.

But, when she looked into his eyes she knew who it was. He had the same eyes that she'd never, ever forget.

Chapter 11

Gray slowed down Frank and Ruth. "Let's stop and watch from Doc's porch. Ruth looks tired," he told Frank. He guided them to the porch and turned to scan the crowd. What Gray really wanted to do was find Erin.

"Hello, Frank. At first I thought you were with Erin until I saw you coming onto the porch with your uncle."

"Hello, Nurse Ellie. Have you seen my wife?"

She nodded. "She was heading down the street towards the sheriff's office. I thought you walked up to her and then realized it was Mr. Langley. He was asking about her earlier. I don't know the whole story but I did point her out to him. He was off the porch and heading towards her."

"Langley? Are you sure?"

Gray's head began to ache. When Erin accused him of telling the whole town about her incident in Memphis, he was offended that she would think he wasn't capable of keeping a secret.

"Yes, she went with him towards Dallas's farm. I think Mr. Langley is renting a room there since the boarding house is full. I know Dallas does that on occasion. I'm sorry, did I do a bad thing?" Nurse Ellie's intent stare made him realize his wife may be in danger.

"Can you keep an eye on these two until I get back?"

"Yes, I'll take them inside for some milk and cookies when the caroling is over. We have a table set up inside for those who can't make it back to the church."

"Thank you. I'll be back soon." He rushed down the stairs and pushed his way through the crowd. The Dallas ranch was right outside of town past the sheriff's office. If anything happened to

Erin, he'd kill whoever was trying to harm her. Why was a Langley here? Not to be friendly, that much he knew.

The sheriff was leaning up against the post. He didn't miss much. "Where are you going in such a hurry, Gray?"

Gray didn't turn from his destination. "My wife may be in danger." Gray began to run now, down the hill at record speed and turned into the lane without thinking twice. He heard the sheriff right behind him.

They covered the long lane at record speed. The trees that lined the road gave off an eerie feel but Gray was on a mission. He wasn't about to let any harm come to his wife.

They made it through the long line of trees to a clearing. The huge house was on the left in a grove while the big barn and several buildings were on the right. Gray skirted the buildings. "I'm not sure where they are."

The sheriff pointed with a grin on his face. "I knew Gertrude would chase him out." He pulled his gun from the holster and pointed it at the man high-tailing it from the barn. A huge goose was flapping her wings and making such loud noises it made Gray's ears hurt.

"Hold up right there!"

The man didn't stop. He ran right past the two and back up the lane with Gertrude following behind.

"Looks like this will be a chase. Go get your wife, Gray. The goose will chase him all the way off the property. Dallas nor Scarlett is here to quiet her down."

Gray didn't think twice before he ran towards the barn. His wife was standing there, hands on her hips, watching Gertrude go after Langley. When she saw Gray, her eyes lit up and she ran to him. He opened his arms and she fell into them. "Erin."

She was shivering in his arms when he took her by her shoulders and pulled her back so he could see if she were all right. "Did he hurt you?"

Turns out the shivers were not from being afraid. She was trying to hold back laughter. "Did you see the goose chase him off. The moment we got to this place, I knew I was no longer in danger."

"I tend to believe you were, Erin. My heart is still beating like a mad man." He took her hand and placed it on his chest."

She smiled up at him. "Jeremiah Langley wanted to take me back to Memphis with him to explain to his mother what he knew all along. When I told him I would not go back, he insisted. He said if I didn't come back he would force me. That's when he pulled a gun and had me come here. I don't think he'd harm me. He was actually on a mission to clear our name."

Gray was confused. "Why would a man come all this way to clear your family name? That does not make sense."

"Because it turns out that his brother had several bastards from his indiscretions. Jeremiah tried to tell his parents that his brother attacked women. He knew the only way to make sure those children would not go without was to prove he was right. I'm not sure why my testimony would make a difference though."

Gray nodded. It all made sense. He gave her another hug and held her for a few minutes longer. "I realize now that if anything had happened to you, I'd have killed him. I know how your father felt that day. It's time to move on from that, Erin. You don't have to feel guilt because a man takes care of his own. It was your father's choice. Not yours."

Erin knew a tear fell when he wiped it away and leaned towards her. "I think I love you, Gray."

He kissed her. "I know I love you, Erin."

*****

"It's Christmas eve. We need a tree."

"Frank, put down the ax. I'll go with you to chop down a tree." Gray walked towards his uncle, his arm reaching for the wooden handle.

"I wanted to surprise my wife and bring back a tree to decorate." Frank looked disappointed when Gray took the ax from him. Gray, on the other hand, looked extremely relieved.

Erin laughed. "We will all go along." She wanted this evening to be special. It had been so long since she had spent this time of year happy. "I'll go get my mother."

The men waited outside while she went to find her mother, who was busy at her sewing machine. Erin peeked in the parlor. "Frank wants to chop down a tree so we can decorate."

"Oh? Frank? Why is he working so late? Tell him to go home to his family."

Erin was worried that her mother's memory was getting worse. Sometimes it was easy to remind her and set her right, but other times she got angry. Erin never knew which mood her mother was going to be in. "Frank is your husband, Mother."

The elder woman stood up and clapped the palms of her hands over her cheeks. "Oh, dear! Why didn't you tell me. I have been waiting all day for him to come home. Where has he been?"

Erin knew it was going to be a long night as she gently reminded her mother what day it was and why everyone was waiting on them. "We better go now, it will be dark soon and then we can't chop down a tree."

That prompted Ruth to fetch her shawl and trudge along to the woods to pick out a tree. It was a fun three hours, but when they got back to the house, Ruth told everyone she was tired and wanted to go to bed. Frank went with her, leaving the two of them alone.

"Would you care for some hot chocolate, Gray?" Erin had ordered some of the Belgian Chocolate from Mr. Dunleavy and had a stash put away for them to enjoy. It was one of the luxuries she insisted upon.

"Yes. Can we sit on the porch?" He topped the tree with a small angel that Ruth had sewn. She had wanted a tree put up ever since they came back from caroling and worked hard for the past twenty-four hours taking material and sewing bells and balls out of leftover material. He stood back and admired his work.

"Yes, go sit down, Gray. I'll get our cups and be right out." She stared at the tree, noticing how crooked it stood in the corner of their parlor. Yet, it was beautiful in her eyes. Just like her family. She prepared the cocoa and hot water and added some cream she had whipped up earlier.

She handed her husband a cup and sat alongside him on the bench. "This is delicious."

"It's very expensive, Erin. We have to talk about spending too much."

She raised a finger to his mouth. "Shh. Not tonight. We are not going to discuss that. Besides, I have a gift for you."

Gray rolled his eyes. "Erin, this is what I'm saying. I asked you not to get me a gift since we are low on funds."

She gave him a shy smile. "Did you buy me a gift, Gray?" She knew the answer, but wanted to hear him say it.

He nodded. "Of course, I did."

Her brow rose. "I think you should not reprimand me if you do the same thing."

He shrugged. "It's Christmas and my duty as your husband to do so."

Erin laughed. "Gray, there are plenty of husbands who don't buy their wives a present when they can't afford to."

"I can't fool you for one minute, can I?" He gave her a loving grin and pulled out a small wrapped package from his pocket.

"I want you to open mine first," Erin told him, taking an envelope out of her pocket. "Please."

"That doesn't seem right that I open it first."

"I insist."

He didn't argue, but tore open the envelope. He blinked several times. "What is this?"

"It's our bank account, Gray. I added your name to my savings. Now you can hire some help around here and don't have to work so hard."

"Erin, how did you get this much money?"

She grinned. "I robbed a stage? No, no, I'm kidding, Gray! The look on your face just now is priceless."

"Never tell a retired Texas Ranger that you robbed a stage. I'm afraid I'd have to turn you in."

She giggled and scooted closer. "Then I'd be in jail and you'd have to raise our children yourself."

"I'd tell them what kind of gun-toting stage robbing mama they had."

Erin flung her head back and laughed. "Oh, Gray, I do love you so much."

"Merry Christmas, Erin. Come closer. I want to kiss you."

"Merry Christmas, Gray. By next year this time, I hope we have a little one to celebrate the holiday with."

He pulled her into his arms, the cups of chocolate forgotten. "I think it's time we start to work on that."

"I agree. Right after I open your present." She pulled back and tore off the paper and twine he had wrapped it with. She opened up the small square box to find a ring with a tiny sparkling diamond in the middle. "It's quite exquisite. But, how were you able -"

This time his finger touched her lips. "Shh. It was my mothers. Now, it belongs to you."

He picked her up in his arms and carried her across the threshold. "Now, my darling, it's time to work on a family."

"The best Christmas present ever."

*****

Thank you for reading Gray and Erin's story in Christmas in Mill Ridge. If you haven't read the book about Dallas and Scarlet and the crazy goose, here's a link to my book in the Bachelor and Babies series, DALLAS:

Dallas: Bachelor's & Babies Available now on Amazon[1] (https://www.amazon.com/Cyndi-Raye-ebook/dp/ B07W1DY1G5)

If you are new to the town of Mill Ridge, you can read about the adventures of some of the town folk in the Brides of Mill Ridge here:

---

1. https://www.amazon.com/Cyndi-Raye-ebook/dp/B07W1DY1G5

Brides of Mill Ridge Box set Volumes 1-6 Available on Amazon NOW![2] (https://www.amazon.com/gp/product/B07NKCHCTB)

Brides of Mill Ridge, is a frontier town about an hours ride from Wichita Falls, the town depicted in the Mail Order Brides of Wichita Falls series. This is a series of six American Historical Romances. You will find many of the characters you've come to love from Wichita Falls show up somewhere in these stories.

An Outlaws Honor - Not everything is the way it seems. Can a heartbroken Elizabeth forgive Noah for leaving her at the worst time of her life? Can Noah win her back, no matter the cost? Never give your heart to an outlaw!

A Reverends Rose - He wasn't what he pretended to be - but then neither was she! Will their hearts be broken when the truth is revealed or will they work through the sea of lies they've both been hiding behind?

The Rangers Redemption - A determined woman with grit - an ex-Texas Ranger with a limp - forced into marriage by a mistaken ordeal! How will they survive?

---

2. https://www.amazon.com/gp/product/B07NKCHCTB

A Doctor's Devotion - A frightened woman hiding a secret - a doctor determined to find the truth - a situation out of control. How bad can it get?

A Teachers Treasure - A treasure hunting teacher - A mysterious handsome stranger - Both searching for a long lost book for different reasons! Will the treasure bring Jennie and Mack together or tear them apart?

A Sister's Sanctuary - A sweet mother with a troubled past - A handsome stranger hiding his past - Can they find sanctuary in Mill Ridge?

All 6 books in one box set for those wanting their stories in on shot!

Available to READ NOW[3] (https://www.amazon.com/gp/product/B07NKCHCTB)

---

3. https://www.amazon.com/gp/product/B07NKCHCTB

Cyndi's Books

Mail Order Brides of Wichita Falls Series
Ruby
Grace
Lily
Charity
Hannah
Rebecca
Sophie
Ellie
Jenna
Leila
Addie (The Final Chapter)
Boxed Set Vol 1
Boxed Set Vol 2
Christmas in Wichita Falls Holiday Book
Brides of Mill Ridge Series
An Outlaws Honor
A Reverend's Rose
The Ranger's Redemption
A Doctor's Devotion
A Teacher's Treasure
A Sister's Sanctuary
Christmas in Mill Ridge
Brides of Mill Ridge Box Set
Sons of Nora White Series
A Bride for Luke

A Bride for Adam
A Bride for Samuel
A Groom for Nora
A Bride for Russell
A Bride for Wesley
A Groom for Widow Young
The Pistol Ridge series
Peg Leg's Princess
Blazes' Beauty
Judge's Jewel
Creed's Confidant
Raven's Rebel
Rider's Renegade
Preacher's Pearl
A Pistol Ridge Scrooge Christmas
The Pistol Ridge Box Set Volume 1
Multi-Author Series Contributions
A Bride for Abel - The Proxy Brides (How Pistol Ridge series started)
A Bride for Calvin - The Proxy Brides (Also part of Pistol Ridge series)
A Bride for Arthur - The Proxy Brides
A Tin Star for Christmas - The Belles of Wyoming
Stealing Her Heart - The Belles of Wyoming
Mercy's Gift - The Belles of Wyoming
Candy Cane Christmas - Ornamental Matchmaker Book #10
An Agent for Carolina - The Pinkerton Match Maker series Book #24
An Agent for Cari - The Pinkerton Match Maker series
Dallas - Bachelor's & Babies series (Set in Mill Ridge)

Viola - Angel Creek Christmas Brides

All of these books & more can be found by visiting Cyndi's Amazon Author Page[1] (https://www.amazon.com/Cyndi-Raye/e/B00ENA1WEG)